W9-AVS-416

SURVIVORS OF
SUICIDE

SURVIVORS OF
SUICIDE

By
Rita Robinson

NEW PAGE BOOKS
A division of The Career Press, Inc.
Franklin Lakes, NJ

Copyright © 2001 by Rita Robinson

All rights reserved under the Pan-American and International Copyright Conventions. This book may not be reproduced, in whole or in part, in any form or by any means electronic or mechanical, including photocopying, recording, or by any information storage and retrieval system now known or hereafter invented, without written permission from the publisher, The Career Press.

Survivors of Suicide

Edited by Nicole DeFelice
Typeset by Nicole DeFelice
Cover design by Melvin L. Harris
Revisions to cover by Lu Rossman/Digi Dog Design
Printed in the U.S.A. by Book-mart Press

To order this title, please call toll-free 1-800-CAREER-1 (NJ and Canada: 201-848-0310) to order using VISA or MasterCard, or for further information on books from Career Press.

The Career Press, Inc., 3 Tice Road, PO Box 687,
Franklin Lakes, NJ 07417
www.careerpress.com
www.newpagebooks.com

Library of Congress Cataloging-in-Publication Data

Robinson, Rita
    Survivors of suicide / by Rita Robinson.— Rev. ed.
    p. cm.
    Includes bibliographical references and index.
    ISBN 1-56414-557-3 (pbk.)
    1. Suicide—Psychological aspects. 2. Bereavement—Psychological aspects. 3. Suicide victims—Family relationships. 4. Suicide—United States. 5. Suicide—Religious aspects—Christianity. I. Title.
    HV6545 .R58 2001
    362.2'8'0973—dc21   2001031515

DEDICATION

For my parents
Mary Elizabeth and Starling Clark Robinson

Acknowledgments

My gratitude to the many survivors who shared their stories with me, and to the mental health professionals and religious leaders who took time to discuss and impart their knowledge so that others may have a more enlightened understanding of suicide and its aftermath. These sharing individuals, minus their titles, which are in the book's text, include: Bem P. Allen, Shahid Athar, Janet B., Alan L. Berman, Ben Zion Bergman, James A. Blumenthal, Carlfred Broderick, Dana Brookins, Robert Carney, Robert Cancro, Mary S. Cerney, Peter Covas, Robert Dawidoff, Leslie Elliott, Gary Emery, Norman Farberow, R. T. D. Farmer, Chip Frye, Robert Gable, Marvin Goodman, Elaine Garcia, Madelyn S. Gould, Phyllis and Covell Hart, Sam Heilig, Paul Hilsdale, David Hoffman, Taffy Hoffman, Mamoru Iga, Ira and Jeanne Jacoves, Nalini Juthani, Gerald Klerman, Monette L., Barry D. Lebowitz, H. Newton Malony, Jean Mathews, Helen Mayberg, Richard T. Monahan, Diane C. Mary Ortega, Michael L. Peck, David P. Phillips, Jane Frances Power, Frederic Rabinowitz, Havanpola Ratanasara, David K. Reynolds, Paul Rohde, Richard J. Seiden, Laurie S., Chris Sekaer, Jan van der Wal, Carol V., T. Wilson, Carol Wold, Adina Wrobleski, and many others who sparked conversations that made me dig for answers.

Contents

Foreword... *13*

Introduction.. *15*

Chapter 1: The Impact, Shock, Grief, and Guilt.................... *23*
  Grief of suicide may be different 23
  Many don't know what to say 25
  The unanswered "why?" 25
  It is normal to grieve 28
  Dealing with insensitive people 31
  Survivors of suicide recover 32
  Fears associated with suicide 33
  The need to grieve 34
  How children grieve 36
  Overcoming depression in grief 37
  Thoughts of suicide 38
  The blame game 39
  Carrying the grief 41
  Allow others to share the grief 42
  Letting go 44

Chapter 2: Survivors Speak Out *47*

Chapter 3: Suicide Myths *75*

   We're all affected by suicide 76

   Placing blame 79

   The myths 79

Chapter 4: Who Commits Suicide? *101*

   Certain groups are at higher risk 103

Chapter 5: Confronting Depression *115*

   What is depression? 118

   Depression is not normal in the elderly 122

   How a depressed brain reacts 122

   Physical illness and depression 124

   Getting help 126

Chapter 6: Historical Perspectives *135*

   Religion and history 136

   Changes in attitude 139

   Beginnings of a new approach 139

   The role of societies in suicide 141

   Changes in help for the survivors 142

   Taboos 143

   Ethics, euthanasia, and technology 143

Chapter 7: Religious Perspectives *147*

   Jewish tradition 148

   Christian tradition 150

   Buddhist tradition 155

   Islamic tradition 157

   Hindu tradition 159

Chapter 8: Preventing Suicide *163*

    Dealing with the pain 164

    Friendship 166

    Stages of suicide 169

    Strengths for suicide prevention 169

    Suicide warning signs 170

    The role of guns in suicide 171

    Prevention targets all areas of society.................... 172

    The goals 175

Chapter Notes *177*

Bibliography *191*

Resources *193*

Index *199*

About the Author *203*

Foreword

Two days after I was given the manuscript of *Survivors of Suicide*, I met a man whose son had killed himself just the week before. He said, "I'm reading a book a friend gave me, and it is helping a little." I was happy to be able to say to him, "I have another book for you. It's not in print yet; you can read my copy." It made me feel a little better to know I was putting something in his hands to help him in the days of grief that were before him.

"Life is difficult." So begins *The Road Less Traveled* by M. Scott Peck. I knew when I read that first sentence that it was a book I wanted to read. I had the same feeling when I began reading *Survivors of Suicide*. This is a book that needs to be read. It is likely that if you are reading this book, someone you know and love tried to, or did, commit suicide. I have been a therapist for nearly 30 years, and I have found that often the best therapy may be to hear and be comforted by someone who has suffered the same trauma.

In this book you will hear from those who have suffered as you have. You will read their stories, and in between the lines, feel their pain, their outrage, their despair, and their hope.

Suicide is a compelling and personal tragedy. It leaves survivors bewildered and confused—and usually guilt-stricken. "Why did they do it?" and "If only I had..." are phrases said over and over again.

Mary had visited in our home just a few days before she got into her car in her garage and turned on the motor. She was a young mother of three children, and when her wonderful husband died suddenly of an unusual illness, she had become depressed. Her doctor had planned to hospitalize her soon. If only we had her stay with us, if only....

Survivors of Suicide is a good and necessary book. You will need it if:

- You have lost someone through suicide.
- Someone you know has tried to harm himself or herself.
- You have contemplated suicide yourself.
- A friend, relative, or acquaintance is a survivor of suicide.
- You are a counselor, clergyperson, or mental health professional.

Comfort comes to us in many and diverse ways. This book has been a comfort to me; I pray it will be so for you.

—Phyllis Hart, Ph.D.,
psychologist and author of *Concurrent Counseling,*
and former Presbyterian minister

Introduction

Every year in the United States, at least 30,000 people kill themselves, and for every death by suicide, there are up to 25 others who attempt suicide. Every suicide touches dozens of acquaintances, friends, and family members.

Only in the past few years has there been a concerted effort to provide help for the survivors—those family and friends left behind in the aftermath of a loved one's self-inflicted death.

Even as doors open, shining rays of hope and light on suicide and its tragic aftermath, the stigmas and misunderstandings continue to dance around the perimeters of our insight. These shadows bring forth the questions that continually plague the survivors: "If only...," "What if...," and the biggie, "Why?"

Existing side by side with enlightenment on suicide's causes, prevention, survivor healing, and effects on society are ignorance, intolerance, and judgment.

Even though various faiths are among the enlightened, and suicidologists and mental health professionals try to get the word out about the true causes of suicide and offer help to the survivors, as many myths exist about suicide as they do about mental disorders as a whole. These myths make it more difficult for survivors to heal from such a devastating loss. It is my belief that only through openness, education, and love can we help the survivors.

We are at the dawn of understanding suicide. In recent years, light has been shed on the causes of someone taking his or her own life through a greater understanding of mental disorders, the availability of scientific techniques to help us see how the brain functions, and increased understanding of the role genetics plays in our lives.

For the first time in the history of the United States, the 1999 yearly health report from the Surgeon General's office included the mental health of the nation. It called for more research and understanding of depression and suicide, which in most cases are linked. The report, in part, concluded that at least 15 percent of children and adolescents have some symptoms of depression and that an estimated 5 percent of children between the ages of 9 and 17 experience full-fledged major depression.

With this widespread interest in the study of depression and suicide will come greater support for those touched by the condition. They will emerge from the shadows possibly with new understandings of why a loved one commits suicide. Yet the definition of suicide will remain the same.

French sociologist Emile Durkheim's definition of suicide, which he penned at the turn of the last century, is still in wide use today among mental health professionals: "The termination of an individual's life resulting directly or indirectly from a positive or negative act of the victim himself, which he knows will produce this fatal result."[1]

Once the causes of this self-inflicted termination of life are better understood, more suicides can be prevented, and when one cannot be prevented, the survivors will have more sources to turn to in order to heal their grief.

This book is written for the survivors, for they are still in the shadows of the emerging enlightenment surrounding suicide. Through their stories recounted on these pages, they make it abundantly clear that they need a community capable of offering support, help, love, and understanding, instead of the age-old taboos, stigmas, half-truths, and ignorance that have, in the past, kept the closet door so tightly shut.

Suicide and its aftermath will eventually receive the enlightenment and understanding accorded Sudden Infant Death Syndrome (SIDS), schizophrenia, and autism. We know now that SIDS is caused by diagnosable physical conditions, where once it was blamed on negligent parents; that schizophrenia is treatable and viewable with brain scans, where once it was blamed on the parents' interaction with their child; and that autism is another genetic condition that manifests itself in a brain condition, where once it was blamed on an unloving mother.

Discussions on suicide prevention, the latest suicide research, history, and views of a variety of faiths are included in this book, but it is the survivor who speaks most eloquently. Each story is unique, yet there is a common thread. The survivors are all thrust into areas of grief that send them to the edge of despair. But by peering over this edge, they sometimes see things that are obscure to others. They become our teachers. Because of their insights, these survivors have the right to demand that our institutions, politicians, philosophers, health professionals, and religious leaders come to grips with suicide.

Taking one's own life is not a single issue. It tugs at the fabric of other social conditions that have long been neglected. It demands our attention and compassion. Lucky are those of us who have not been directly touched by suicide, but we owe our thoughtfulness and compassion to those who have peered over the abyss.

When I wrote one survivor whose 21-year-old son had committed suicide, asking permission for an interview, she answered, "I would be happy to speak to you—in hopes it will help other people. It helps my healing to help others to understand."

Her words were echoed by a 29-year-old man whose brother had committed suicide. "Talking about it might help someone else who's going through a similar situation," he said.

There is no appropriate moment in time that lessens the impact of hearing that a loved one or an acquaintance has committed suicide. The event is shattering at any hour of the day or night. It violates the strongest of emotions and urges. It violates our purpose—the will to survive that is programmed into our genes. Nonetheless, at some point in many people's lives, this menacing stranger will grip their hearts and rip apart their emotions.

Unlike other forms of death, which are followed by established patterns of grief, suicide leaves the survivor wallowing in uncharted areas. However, healing usually follows the same patterns as other types of death.

Despite headline-making suicides, and the fact that thousands of people commit suicide each year, when it hits close to home, people feel as if they're the only ones who have ever been touched so powerfully by suicide—a singular entity engulfed with overwhelming feelings of grief, shame, anger, guilt, and frustration.

Until they are touched by it, most people do not give suicide a second thought. They seem to prefer to believe that it is a rare occurrence. I'm constantly reminded of a conversation I had with a young professor of journalism. We were discussing writing and I mentioned that I was working on this book.

"Seems like your market would be quite limited," she said. "I've never known anyone who committed suicide."

Not wanting to shatter her youthful naivete completely, I only mentioned that in the United States more than 11 people per 100,000 commit suicide each year.

Suicide is a stranger to no race, creed, religion, age group, income bracket, or education level, and people have been taking their own lives since the beginning of recorded history.

The "why" of suicide is the big question—both for researchers and those left behind. I've seldom met a survivor who could pinpoint the reason for a person's taking his or her own life. The unanswered question is one that leaves people in turmoil. Even when a suicide note is left it rarely touches on the true cause. The victim's thinking process is too distorted by then. Additionally, survivors constantly question the "why" of their own reactions to the suicide.

Janet B., a former volunteer at a suicide prevention center in Los Angeles, recalls that four years after her brother's suicide she was driving down the freeway and began crying and screaming about the incident. She had kept her feelings of rage, anger, grief, and guilt bottled up for so many years that even though she had worked at the center for two years, she still wasn't over her own personal trauma. Janet is not an exception.

Although some research indicates that survivors of suicide recover at about the same pace as those who lose a loved one to any unanticipated death, the mythology of suicide tells them that they should suffer longer and differently.

Some researchers, however, are saying that survivors might need a different type of counseling in addition to grief therapy, one that addresses the trauma of losing a loved one to suicide, which can be likened to posttraumatic stress disorder.

It is natural for people who have lost a loved one in an accident or from a serious illness to grieve periodically throughout their lives, but it softens through the years, and so it does for the survivors of suicide. We also grieve periodically for elderly loved ones who have died from natural causes. A highly paid computer expert who travels worldwide, and who lost her mother three years ago, was talking about what she wanted to do with the rest of her life when she suddenly became teary eyed and said, "I want to talk to my mother about this."

However, life may never return to what we perceive as normal when we lose someone to suicide. One woman said that after the death of her daughter by suicide she had to "carve out a new normal." However, it may be the first hours, days, and months after the death that create such a muddied mosaic for the survivors of suicide.

When Janet received news of her brother's suicide she requested that her fellow workers not send flowers or cards or offer to help, as they had done the previous year when her mother had died. "And I don't know why I did that," she said. "I don't know whether it was because if they didn't do anything I wouldn't have to deal with it, or if there was a part of me that was thinking, 'He doesn't deserve the same as my mother.' I don't know to this day."

Not only is the grieving family member or friend left with a plethora of unanswered questions, he or she must also face the ignorance of some friends and acquaintances who believe much of the mythology of suicide.

I was once discussing suicide with some acquaintances when one of them, a woman, said she had a friend who had been married twice and both husbands had committed suicide.

The gentleman sitting with us snidely remarked, "Wonder what she's doing to drive them to suicide?"

It was like talking to a blank wall trying to explain to him that no one directly causes another person to take his or her own life.

One woman, who claims to be a born-again Christian, and whose stepfather committed suicide several years ago, said, "Well, we know what happened to him. He went straight to hell."

Another woman adamantly states that people who commit suicide are selfish and doomed to hell. A Native American woman attended services at a local church for the brother of a friend only to hear the minister condemn the victim and offer no solace to the family. The Native American woman had the courage and conviction to stand up during the services and say that the minister was wrong, and that of course a loving God will embrace the tortured soul who committed suicide and will wrap His arms around the survivors.

Most religious bodies today, while not endorsing suicide, take a more enlightened view. The idea of punishing someone who has already been living an internal hell-on-earth seems rather cruel, especially for the survivors.

There was a time when people who attempted suicide were treated far worse than criminals, and families of suicide victims were disowned by a community. That legacy may be past, but the stigma and taboo still weave through society like a river of poison.

What is significant is that never before in our history has there been such an interest in the cause and prevention of depression and suicide. Society is demanding answers, clear understanding, and more gentle treatment of the suicide victim and the survivors.

Through these pages, many of the myths commonly associated with suicide will be dispelled. Offered instead will be some of the truths that are changing the shapes and the shadows that have stayed hidden for so long in the closet.

Much is being done on the positive side for potential suicide victims and survivors of suicide. Mental health professionals, governments, individuals, schools, social service organizations, scientists, and religious bodies are working toward saving more lives from the abyss of suicide. Although the affliction has not been eliminated, and probably never will be, it is being addressed by more and more groups and individuals with understanding, enlightenment, and compassion.

Chapter 1

The Impact, Shock, Grief, and Guilt

Suicide hits below the belt. We are often somewhat prepared for the deaths of elderly parents or friends and relatives with serious diseases, and they too are painful, but we are seldom aware that suicide will touch us.

Many support groups have been established for widows and widowers, for those whose loved ones have been murdered, and for parents whose children meet untimely deaths, but support groups for survivors of suicide are a newer pehnomenon. Most of the growth in the past decade has come from those in the healing professions who became aware of how an individual suicide impacts dozens of other people.

Grief of suicide may be different

Thanks to the efforts of people like Dr. Elisabeth Kubler-Ross, one of the pioneers in the hospice movement who helped enlighten the public on death and dying, death is now seen as a more natural part of life, but suicide is not. Although the stages of grief have been explored and have become universal, they come in different forms when death is caused by suicide.

In any type of bereavement, people may experience emotions that range from alarm, disbelief, and denial to anger and guilt. Finding a source of comfort and eventually adjusting to the loss become important goals. When suicide is the cause of death, however, these stages are taken apart, turned upside down and backwards, and shaken as if by an earthquake.

Those left behind, the survivors of the suicide victim, tend to experience a very complicated form of bereavement, partly due to the combination of the sudden shock, the unanswered question of "Why?" and possibly the trauma of discovering or witnessing the suicide. Survivors' grief reactions can become even more exacerbated by insensitive responses from the community.[1]

Although many suicide survivors initially experience frequent feelings of rejection, responsibility, and more total grief reactions, as well as increased levels of shame and perceived stigmatization,[2] it's believed that the majority eventually recover at about the same speed as others responding to the death of a loved one. This is not to say that the death won't be viewed as different, and that some may not have more problems during the grieving period, but this is true of survivors of loved ones in any type of death. Some researchers say that survivors of suicide can't be distinguished from those other survivors two to four years after the death of a loved one. This is even true of children whose parents die from suicide, compared with those whose parents die from cancer.[3] At the same time, siblings who lose a brother or sister to suicide don't show any increased risk for depression, posttraumatic stress disorder, or other negative conditions after three years. Neither do the fathers of the deceased child. Mothers, however, still show signs of depression after three years.[4]

When a person loses a spouse to an accident or illness, well-meaning friends and family often spend time with the bereaved, just listening to him or her. However, people shy away from suicide survivors. Frequently they don't know how to begin a conversation with the bereaved. One very close friend of a woman whose young son had committed suicide said she didn't go visit the woman because, "I just didn't know what to say."

Many don't know what to say

When I attended the funeral of my friend Beverly, who committed suicide several years ago, I too was stuck for something to say to the survivors—the woman's grown children whom I had known since they were small. The words spoken at her service had no meaning to me. It was as if I was taking part in a daydream, half awake and half asleep. Nothing seemed real.

To this day, I don't think of Beverly as dead. She had been my next-door neighbor when our children were young. I remember her as being wonderful with her own five children, and she always had a house full of other people's kids.

Her first husband left with another woman three days before Christmas one year, but Beverly eventually remarried when her children were in their teens. The marriage seemed happy and stable, and when I visited Beverly in her new home, life seemed better than the earlier years. But a few years later, after her children were grown and married, I received a call from her husband telling me that Beverly, who worked for a diet doctor, had been missing for the weekend. They had found her body in the office where she worked. She had gone there on a Friday, taken a quantity of pills, and was found dead Monday morning when the staff came to work.

Several years have passed since her death, and to this day it does no good for me to try to understand why she did it. She had a great sense of humor and it was fun just being with her. The death left me with a feeling of emptiness, and I wish now that I could talk to the family and could have taken a more enlightened part in her funeral.

The unanswered "Why?"

I know I can never know why Beverly committed suicide or what was going on in her mind during those last few hours, minutes, and seconds. But survivors of suicide always ask themselves that question, and they are frequently asked by well-meaning friends, "Why do you suppose he or she did this terrible thing?"

One woman, whose daughter had committed suicide, wrote Ann Landers, saying, "When something like this happens, there is a tremendous guilt among family members and everyone close. The most painful question for me was, 'Why did she do it?' Every time I am asked it makes me feel that she would still be with us somehow, if only I had paid more attention or if I had stayed home that day, and a million other ifs. Just thinking about it now makes the pain come back, and it's as bad as the day it happened.

"What I want to shout to everyone is that 'I DON'T KNOW!' Don't they think if I had seen it coming I would have moved heaven and earth to prevent it? The girl was my heart and soul."

Perhaps those who ask the question, "Why did they do it?" are trying to find answers themselves, feeling that those close to them might also be vulnerable. The death of a young person, for instance, frightens all parents.

"The suicide death of a loved one makes us reevaluate our own lives," said the sister of a young man who took his own life. "I fainted when I first heard about it. I kept thinking it was a joke. Sometimes I think it still hasn't happened."

Suicide is simply not in our frame of reference. Yet, whenever it's mentioned, it becomes evident that all are touched by this tragedy.

Everyone seems to have a suicide story. Often it's been kept buried for years because families don't feel comfortable discussing something that has, in the past, been such a taboo subject.

A contractor who was working on my house after a fire destroyed a bedroom asked me what I was writing. When I told him about the book, he stepped in the doorway, head down and said, "My brother committed suicide."

Tears welled in the eyes of this former Marine, father of nine children, as he related the experience that had occurred more than 10 years ago. Before he continued his story, he apologized for his tears.

"We'd gone drinking together after work, and I always wondered if we hadn't done that, [if] he might still be alive. He had a drinking problem..."

My daughter called in tears one day. "Mom, what can we do? Paula just committed suicide."

Paula worked in a medical office near my daughter's place of employment. Paula had previously asked one of the other workers to teach her how to give injections. The co-worker complied and a few days later Paula gave herself a fatal drug injection. She left two children.

Not only did Paula leave family and friends to grieve without the anchor of clearly knowing why she died, but the co-worker is left with the guilt that somehow, if she hadn't shown her how to give injections, Paula might still be alive. The co-worker won't be alone, however. Paula's family and friends will most likely conjure up their own feelings of guilt, despite the knowledge that once the deed is done, no one is responsible but the suicide victim. We can also ask just how responsible the suicide victim is when research shows that people can be genetically predisposed to depression that can lead to suicide. They can also have brain abnormalities in cases of mental disorders, such as schizophrenia and bipolar disorder, and what's more, victims often present themselves as calm and collected, especially as they move closer to the actual deed. A life trauma can also trigger depression that can lead to suicide, especially if a genetic predisposition to depression exists.

One father whom I interviewed about the death of his young son was particularly open about his overwhelming feelings of grief, and acknowledged that men have a tougher time dealing with the suicide of a loved one because they have been taught to contain their emotions. I told him about another father who had stated flatly years after his son's suicide, "It doesn't bother me that much. I felt no guilt."

"He's lying," was the first father's comment.

Another survivor, who worked at a suicide prevention center, mentioned her work during a social occasion, and a man at the table said, "Oh, my father committed suicide." His wife's head spun around as she said, "You've never said that to anyone outside the family!"

Sometimes a suicide is more difficult to talk about with family members. Janet B., whose brother committed suicide, avoided talking to her father about it for more than three years.

"I was afraid it would upset him," she says. But during a trip when she called her father to let him know the plane was taking off, she confided to him, "I just want you to know that what happened to Mike wasn't your fault." Janet recalls a long silence on the other end of the telephone and then her father replied, "Well, I worked that out a long time ago and I know it wasn't." There was another long pause and then in a little voice her father asked, "How do you know it wasn't my fault?"

Janet acknowledges that she still wants to defend her brother, and defend her family. Once when giving a speech about her brother to raise money for a research grant, she realized most of it was a defense of her brother. "I felt the need to say my brother wasn't crazy. He wasn't on drugs and he hadn't been a failure. I wanted to tell them what a good family we came from."

Her story emphasizes why we're often shocked over many suicides. They don't fit anticipated patterns. Some people have lives filled with horror and they go on. Others have seemingly wonderful lives, and they end them in suicide.

It is normal to grieve

Often when suicide is mentioned, people will at first shake their heads and say something like, "It's never touched my life." Then on reflection, they might add, "Come to think of it, I had an aunt who committed suicide, but no one ever talked about it," or "I had a neighbor who shot himself, but it never affected me."

The truth is, few of us will escape the shadow of suicide.

We can choose to ignore it, or we can grasp the emotions to our bosom in order to feel the deep grief and sorrow that can make us more fully alive.

It is normal to grieve.

Psychotherapist Paul Hilsdale, now deceased, once shared with me part of a letter that he wrote to a grieving family whose son had committed suicide:

> The element of suicide, I know, distorts your suffering, making it even more unbearable. How you must be blaming yourselves for his action. As a psychotherapist, I'm constantly reminded of the destructive power of guilt. And as a Buddhist-Christian, I know that one of our lifelong tasks is the gradual elimination of judgment (and self-condemnation). The jewel-self, the diamond that we were each given at birth, seems to need such a final polishing—a cleansing away of judgment, till what is shines through the dust of what we would want to be.
>
> Recently I came across a poem by Rexroth, describing his reaction to the death of his wife, Andree. It begins: "My sorrow is so wide/I cannot see across it;/And so deep I shall never/Reach the bottom of it."
>
> I would not want to take from you that sense of immensity and finitude—for your feelings are part of your essential diamond and rainbow. So I wrote with no expectation of mending your broken hearts, but only to let you know that you have understanding and caring companions way out here in California.

Although the stages of grief vary in intensity and don't always follow in a particular order, it is normal to have feelings of anger and rage when someone takes his or her own life. These same feelings also present themselves when death is by natural or accidental causes.

I remember attending a grief support group for widows and widowers as a reporter. One woman arrived late and immediately announced, "I don't know why I'm here. It's depressing to be around all these sad people."

She proceeded to add, "My husband died only last week, and maybe I'm not ready for this."

She sat a few moments listening to some of the other people, jumped up, headed for the door and shouted, "None of you have problems like me. My husband left me with everything to do, and I don't know how to do any of it. I wish he were here just so I could scream at him for the fix he left me in."

Following her outburst she left.

The facilitator then asked how many had felt anger when their spouses died. All the participants raised their hands. None of the deceased spouses had committed suicide. Rather, they had died of natural causes, prolonged illnesses, or accidents. It's important to realize that the survivors of suicide go through the grieving process in similar fashion to those who lose loved ones to other causes. Even if the initial grief is more intense, there may not be more guilt among suicide survivors, as is commonly believed, although there may be greater feelings of anger because the person has taken his or her own life. But, other forms of death also create anger and guilt.

The parents of a child who commits suicide will often direct their anger at others—an ex-spouse, other relatives, the authorities. One woman who lost a son said that when she would read in the newspaper about a young man who had been involved in a crime, she would ask angrily, "Why isn't he dead instead of my son?"

Survivors of suicide may try to spend more time by themselves, and probably will avoid people who bring up intense reactions in them. For example, if someone is blaming them for the death, they will naturally want to avoid that person. They are often extremely sensitive to what other people have to say.

Survivors are particularly sensitive to people who give their own interpretations without having the facts of the deceased person's life, to people who point blame, and to those who ask whether the person left a note and what it said.

When Dana Brookins gave the eulogy at the funeral of a young man who had committed suicide, she began with, "There is no blame here." Years later, one of the sisters of the young man reminded Brookins of her remarks. "Somehow," recalled

Brookins, "I think her mentioning it was more profound than just a thanks. I can only imagine the sorrow she felt for her parents when Richard died."

But other survivors, as in the case of an accidental death, are also assaulted by insensitive people with remarks such as, "This might not have happened if you had been there."

Regardless of what causes a death, the loved ones left behind need support and love, not blame.

Dealing with insensitive people

I once read a letter to the editor in a local newspaper in response to an article about a woman with Alzheimer's who had committed suicide. The woman was living with her daughter's family, and it was they who had been caring for her for years. They were devastated. The woman writing the letter in response to the article, however, said that if the family had taken better care of the woman, watched over her better, she wouldn't have committed suicide.

At the time, I became enraged at the insensitivity of the woman who wrote the letter to the editor. Obviously, she had no awareness of the mental states of some Alzheimer's patients, or what it takes to care for them. Not all Alzheimer's patients are subdued or simply forgetful. Many become quite violent toward others and themselves. I was doubly enraged because my own mother, who had died of Alzheimer's years before, had attempted suicide. Twice, I had been forced to place her in a psychiatric unit for a few days—once when she attempted suicide by locking herself in the bathroom and slashing her wrists, and another time when she threatened suicide.

She had been the most gentle of women. She had never raised her voice, never sworn at anyone or anything. Yet, she attacked attendants and bit a dentist. Her outbursts happened only occasionally, were not lasting, and subsided as she got further into her disease.

Insensitive people like the letter writer are the ones who heap additional pain and grief on the family and friends left behind when someone commits suicide. Survivors of non-suicide deaths don't generally encounter the insensitivity of others to the degree that suicide survivors do. But if, for instance, survivors have had a fight with their loved one before an accidental death, they have similar feelings of guilt and heightened sensitivity to the comments of others. This sense of unfinished business is a common reaction to any unexpected death, not just a death by suicide.

Survivors of suicide recover

Jan van der Wal, M.D., of Leiden University in the Netherlands, who has studied grief reactions of suicide survivors, says, "The most remarkable conclusion from our study is that the general assumption of pathology and extreme distress in survivors of suicide is not well founded.

"The assumption that suicide generally has devastating consequences for survivors finds no support in our findings. Contrary to the suggestion that suicide is the most stressful cause of death, we found that traffic fatalities cause even more difficulties with detachment from the deceased than suicides."[5]

Van der Wal also says that suicide doesn't lead to a relatively complicated process of social adjustment, although he adds that the research isn't meant to minimize the severity of bereavement. It just shouldn't be exaggerated in the case of suicide. He says an expectation that suicide should provide more devastating effects than other forms of death can lead survivors to worry unnecessarily. It can also cause caregivers, those who might be assisting a bereaved person, to become overanxious.

Van der Wal's emphasis is: If society expects a suicide survivor to be more devastated than survivors of other forms of death, it becomes a self-fulfilling prophecy.

Adina Wrobleski, late author of *Suicide Survivors: A Guide for Those Left Behind*, said that the greatest need of survivors is reassurance that what they are going through is normal. Some of what they go through may be slightly different than that caused by other forms of death, such as thoughts of their own suicide, but it has nothing to do with the length of time it takes to recover.

Wrobleski began her studies on suicide following the death of her stepdaughter, who shot herself. She said that most survivors of suicide have trouble concentrating, a majority have sleeping difficulties, they feel guilty and angry, and often dream of the deceased. A majority of survivors of suicide also see the death scene in their minds, worry that someone else will die, believe they have seen the person who died, and forget for a moment that the person is dead.

Grieving people of all sorts have panic attacks, headaches, stomachaches, and back pain. Survivors of suicide, however, sometimes have fleeting thoughts of their own suicides, or worry that others in the family will develop a mental illness.

Fears associated with suicide

Wrobleski wrote in the journal *OMEGA*, "There are many fears experienced by suicide survivors. I think the trauma of suicide death forces people to a vivid consciousness of their own death and the potential of everyone's suicide death. Because they are not really suicidal, these fleeting thoughts are frightening and are examples of the 'crazy' thoughts one can have. Another is the fear of mental illness once it has occurred in the family. Still another fear is an apprehension that 'someone else will die.'"[6]

Carol V., a Nevada writer and mother, said she used to worry periodically that she might be suicidal like her sister, who took her own life at the age of 35. She not only worried about herself, but about her children, because there is the possibility of a genetic predisposition to the bipolar disorder that led to her sister's suicide.

The authors of *New Hope for People with Bipolar Disorder* indicate that because of increased research, genetic vulnerability to bipolar illness will be greatly diminished within the next five years. Genetic markers will help diagnose and treat certain mental illnesses.[7]

Eileen Simpson, a New York psychotherapist and author of *Orphans, Real and Imaginary*, lost her mother when she was 1 year old and her father when she was 7. She says that she didn't come to terms with it until she was middle-aged, following the death of her second husband, to whom she'd been married for 20 years. She says that by not grieving properly over her mother's death, she prolonged her grief over her husband's death.[8]

The need to grieve

Young and old alike need to grieve over losses in order for healing to take place.

Dana Brookins recalls that when her friend's 26-year-old son committed suicide, her friend would sit in the first floor of her home and talk for a few minutes, then excuse herself. She would go upstairs and Dana could hear her pacing back and forth, wailing as she had never heard anyone do before. "She would return anywhere from 15 minutes to an hour later and sit down and talk a little more, and then she would go through the same process," Brookins remembers.

The open expression of grief is one key to recovery, as the following story, shared by Jean M. less than a year after her son committed suicide, indicates.

"It's just sort of the ultimate. You worry about your kids getting home safely in a car. You're so happy when they reach 18. All your life, as parents, you learn not to hang on to your kids. You want them to survive.

"You sort of rationalize, and everyone says you did what you could. But in your heart, you can think of a lot of things that maybe you should have done, and you felt, after all, you raised a child so that you wouldn't take care of it forever. You raise them to be able to get out of the nest and take care of themselves.

"And this [the suicide] is the ultimate failure."

Jean realized that she would have periods of mourning for her son the rest of her life. They eased with time, but the pain stayed with her always, just as it does for anyone who loses a son or daughter to any form of death.

I recount Jean's story here in some detail because she was

able to face her son's suicide immediately, and she went on to enrich her life and the lives of others immeasurably. I refer to hers as the "Blue Blanket" story, and it symbolizes the grieving process.

Jean was the single mother of three grown children, including the son who committed suicide following a successful concert tour in the Soviet Union and Asia with the musical group Hiroshima.

At about midnight, her former husband, a judge, called her at her home in a California seaside town, about 80 miles from where he lives. He asked that she get a friend or neighbor to come over immediately and stay with her until he could get there. Then he told her over the phone that the police had just notified him of their son's suicide.

From the moment of the telephone call and throughout the next two weeks, Jean was kept busy making arrangements, dealing with and responding to friends and acquaintances. "Those were the easiest times because I was busy all the time," she recalled. "You are in such a state of shock and there are things to do, like getting ready for the service. You're sort of insulated. It's later, when it all sinks in... when the insulation wears off....

"I was warned about this and it helped. A friend whose daughter had died suddenly of appendicitis told me, 'This is a piece of cake compared to what you're going to go through later.' It wasn't a cruel thing she told me. The love was just pouring out. And it helped."

As predicted, a week later, Jean was lying on the bathroom floor or in the hallway crying. "I'm glad I was warned," she said.

Because the suicide was reported in the papers, strangers responded with sympathy, she recalled. At no time did she ever consider hiding the fact that her son had committed suicide. "It didn't bother me to have it reported," she said.

"We have to accept a certain amount of rottenness in life, and then go on from there," Jean said. She credits that attitude, plus the fact that she can cry a lot without feeling guilty, with helping pull her through.

Friends and family did the rest. Whenever Jean returned home she found that friends had filled the house with fresh fruit and flowers. One evening a friend presented Jean with a soft, puffy, blue comforter. "I thought this might help keep you warm when you're feeling down," the friend said. From that day on, Jean used the blue blanket to snuggle up in whenever she was depressed—and she cried.

Jean said she cried for days at first. "And it helped," she said. Eventually she could go a couple of weeks without crying. "But something small may happen and then I cry. It's uncanny how the pain can be almost as sharp now when I get in one of the crying fits. It's such total grief that it's as bad as it was two weeks after his death. It doesn't happen as often or as long, but it was an enormous type of grief—the wracking of the body. I don't see how it could be any worse," she said.

Jean would take the blanket to the bedroom or the closet or the bathroom and just lie on the floor with the lights out in the fetal position with the blanket over her head.

She knew instinctively it was good for her, she said.

How children grieve

It isn't only adults who experience the grief process, though it has often been assumed that children don't feel grief with the same intensity and understanding as adults. In fact, surviving children are often neglected following the death of a loved one. According to Christina Sekaer, M.D., psychiatrist and faculty member in the department of psychiatry at New York University Medical Center and the William Alanson White Institute, children do mourn, but perhaps in a different way, one that has been overlooked.

Sekaer says that a redefinition of mourning specific to children of each age is needed, as many researchers believe children lack the ego strength and development to tolerate intense pain and therefore cannot carry out the work of mourning.[9] She says that in order for children to mourn they need adult help to understand the fact of a death and to correct their misunderstandings as they develop. The child, even with adult help, cannot understand reality beyond his or her cognitive level.

Children may say, "Mommy's gone to heaven," but they may not understand the finality of death. They may distort the event, says Sekaer. Children are particularly susceptible to feeling shame when returning to school after the suicide of a loved one, which means that they may need additional help in dealing with the grieving process, rather than being shunted in the belief that they don't understand what has happened.

Overcoming depression in grief

Some mental health professionals believe that depression is a natural part of grief, and that if it isn't experienced, the person is simply repressing it. The short-lived depressive state, however, normally doesn't develop into a major depressive illness.

In grieving for the death of a loved one, a person needs to reach a state of acceptance and to resolve conflicts related to grieving in order to complete the bereavement.[10] This may be tougher on survivors of suicide. There is simply more conflict to deal with, and often a plethora of unanswered questions.

To fight the whirlwind of depression that can encircle the grieving, Jean's friends encouraged her to exercise. One of her daughters forced her to go swimming every day.

The swimming, walking, and running may have helped relieve some of Jean's depression. Neurophysiological studies indicate a tendency for a depressed person to have inappropriate levels of certain chemicals (such as serotonin and norepinephrine) in the brain that affect the neurotransmission of electrochemical signals from one brain nerve cell to another. These signals affect thoughts, behavior, and emotions. Exercise alters the chemical balance in a positive way.

Writing about the grief can be another source of help. Although writing about the grief of anyone who dies, whether from natural causes or even a homicide, has proven helpful, it can be particularly beneficial for the survivors of suicide.[11]

Thoughts of suicide

Survivors of suicide may have fleeting thoughts of suicide themselves. Those thoughts are a natural result of grief and of the fact that suicide has been introduced into their own frame of reference, where it hadn't been previously. In some cases, however, the survivor may also have a genetic predisposition to depression and suicide.

Janet B., mentioned earlier, believes that suicide in a family opens doors that are best left closed. "I had this feeling for two years, before I started to talk about it—I'm Italian and German and I have a temper, and I slam doors and stuff—and I was terrified that in one of those fits of temper I was going to run out and buy a gun and shoot myself because my brother did. That's one of the reasons why I wanted to get a support group started, because I believe that 'post-vention' can be prevention too."

Jean, however, said she never thought of committing suicide, but that she did wish a couple of times that she would never ever wake up again.

"When I went to bed at night I had the two-button stage. One button would say, 'You're going to have to wake up and face the world in the morning,' and the other button would say that 'You're never going to have to wake up again.' I think at that time I would have pushed the never-wake-up button."

Jean talked about the double guilt she carried when she began to enjoy life again. "There's a guilt about what you have failed to give him. And then, also, you do feel a little guilty about enjoying your life. Because you allowed this awful thing to happen to your son you shouldn't be able to enjoy your own life.

"You have to live with the fact of ambivalence in your thinking that it might not be your fault. When I was first coming out into the real world again, I was able to be with people and enjoy myself. But at the same time, I would come home and cry and cry. I couldn't reconcile the two emotions. I remember saying to my daughter that one of them had to be false. Either when I'm out having a good time, it's phony, because I'm really grieving. And when I was grieving, I'd say, 'What about the time I was out having a good time?' They're both real. What you're trying to do is to survive. You have very conflicting answers that come to you. And you get very depressed yourself. There is so much going wrong and it is so hard to survive. Life is that way. But you don't entirely believe it. And yet, the minute you start thinking about all that beauty out there, and you go and have a wonderful walk and everything is so glorious—then that is depressing too because it is all denied that person you love—that person who wasn't able to balance his life.

"It's too much to grasp. I don't think ever in my life I will be able to understand it. It is fruitless. You really want to know what happened. But you know you never will. He had so much promise. Was so kind. And was so miserable."

Jean wondered if she will ever get over the occasional thought that her son took his life because she was a bad mother. It's as if, on some level, there is an instinctual assumption that she must have been bad or he wouldn't have died, she said. And there are moments when she wondered if other people believed she was a bad mother.

"You sort of feel stamped as a failure as a parent. But that's in your mind. I never got that from anyone else," she said.

The blame game

Mary S. Cerney, a psychologist formerly of the Menninger Foundation in Topeka, Kansas, said survivors of suicide go through much more guilt than the average grieving person. They wonder how they have contributed to the suicide, and they often think society will blame them. As van der Wal pointed out, this could be a self-fulfilling prophecy, because it's expected, rather than a reality.

Whatever the cause of this guilt, most survivors have it in one form or another. "Guilt," says Janet B. "That's the biggie. I still have it. At least I can help some people now because I couldn't help my brother. I still believe that if he had said something, and we could have gotten him through the next month, maybe he wouldn't have killed himself."

In talking with other survivors—sisters, brothers, friends, mothers, fathers, spouses—they all occasionally ask the question, "Was I somehow to blame because I was a bad mother, father, sister, brother, friend, or spouse?"

Even those who should be trained to help sometimes can't resist placing blame. I interviewed one such person, a specialist in childhood suicide and depression. After I recounted the death of Jean's son, he remarked, "Well, obviously, it was the parents' fault. When a child commits suicide, it's the parent's fault," he reiterated.

Stunned, I argued that the son was 26 years old and had been close to his parents. I proceeded to tell him about how the father had taken his vacation one summer with his son after the boy had said at about age 16 that he wanted to hitchhike to San Francisco. The father, a very dignified-looking judge, said, "Okay, but I'm going with you." The two hitchhiked the more than 900 miles round-trip together.

The psychologist then placed blame on the fact that the youth was a musician. "They're all kind of strange," he said.

Though disenchanted with this particular psychologist, I then explained how the son was a serious musician from a musical family. "Does this doom someone?" I asked.

He backed off again and said that perhaps the youth was mixed up in drugs, or was a homosexual, or was despondent over a bad love, which he said are all possible contributing factors to suicide, although these conditions aren't the actual "cause" of suicide.

At no time did this particular psychologist show the slightest sympathy, love, understanding, or humility that most professionals exhibit.

When seeking professional help if and when it's needed, look around and don't feel you have to stay with the first counselor or therapist you find.

Dana, a friend who heard of my disenchantment with the psychologist who wanted to place blame, is an award-winning children's book author. She wrote me a note saying, "When anyone starts casting blame for suicide, he/she had better look in all directions. A friend of mine, a homosexual, was just shot and killed last week in a boxcar. Whose fault was that? His parents, the environment, society, his genes, the transient (a former mental patient) who shot him? I think all of them were responsible.

"What parent among us can cast the first stone?

"There's very little room for the fragile ones in our society, the ones who need to be held up more than people can hold them up. Sure, the parents had some part in it. So did Oswald, and Nixon, or Von Braun, and the first guy who ever owned a slave. We just don't have much room in this society or tolerance for our butterflies."

Survivors don't need to be judged or blamed when a catastrophe like suicide enters their lives. They need the support of people who give them blue blankets. They need people, nonjudgmental friends, because they're not dealing in theories. They don't have the luxury of speculating on why the person killed him or herself. The deed has already been done. They are dealing with instant pain. Pain that begins the moment they receive the telephone call or discover the body, pain that will stay with them in some small portion of their hearts for the rest of their lives.

Carrying the grief

Pain can engulf anyone who loses a loved one, regardless of the cause of death. And a parent losing a child seems to be among the most painful and long lasting.

Tears still occasionally come into the eyes of a friend who lost a son, a policeman, in the line of duty 20 years ago. After eight years, another friend whose grown daughter was killed by a drunken driver still can't watch the operas on video she and her daughter used to watch together. Another mother grieves silently over a child who died at birth 12 years ago.

One woman accompanies me on a walk because she's heard that I've written a book on suicide. Her daughter committed suicide, and years later she still has no answers. Near the end of the walk, when I ask her, she acknowledges that the daughter was manic-depressive. But she isn't ready for that connection yet. Ironically, some whose loved ones commit suicide are as confused about mental illness as they are about suicide. Often, they don't want to acknowledge mental illness in the family because of the stigma attached to it, which carries its own type of grief.

Grief is a natural part of life, and therefore not one to smother. It can be carried in small places of the heart after the initial grieving period. When it becomes the central focus of the life, long after the death, though, is it unhealthy, and professional help may be necessary to lay it to rest.

"Great grief makes sacred those upon whom its hand is laid. Joy may elevate, ambition glorify, but only sorrow can consecrate," wrote Horace Greely. Sir Aubrey de Vere, an 18th-century poet, wrote, "Grief should be like joy, majestic, sedate, confirming, cleansing, equable, making free, strong to consume small trouble, to command great thought, grave thought, thoughts lasting to the end."

Allow others to share the grief

Although you may feel that you want to be alone, it often helps to allow others to share the grief.

Looking back, Jean said she would never forget the help given her by family and friends. But she believes that the survivors, as well, can help those who are supporting them.

"As a survivor you must know that it may be difficult for some of your friends to know what to do," she noted.

"You must know how impotent your friends feel. You must realize that they don't know what to do. It's awkward for them. And you don't mind. You try to put them at ease and help them because they're trying to imagine what you're going through. But they can't quite imagine how awful it is. But they can come close.

"Popping in on people [the survivors] is okay. And calling, although sometimes I didn't answer. But I had the choice. Sometimes it would be 3 p.m., in the middle of the afternoon, and I would have my robe on. And I wouldn't want to answer the door, but I did. And it was someone who said, 'Let's go take a walk on the beach.' Or 'Let's do this'... and it helped.

"I don't know how you can instruct people to be that sensitive. My friends just seemed to know. Just leave it up to the bereaved person and take a clue from them. Don't push a discussion. My friends were so accepting of my mood. Accepting and helpful."

Eventually, Jean realized she had to get on with life. "You have to get in a situation where your mind is on something else, the mechanics of living. Perhaps a job. You have to be distracted from this thing that happened. If you just sit and think about the horror of it, you would be gone.

"I didn't think I would ever go back to the choral [a group she had recently joined]. How could I walk into that room? They all knew. Four months later, my daughter talked me into going. I liked singing and they were all nice to me. After I got there, I just barely made it through the evening. I didn't think it was going to be a bummer, but it was. I said I'd never go back. But my daughter made me go back and it became easier."

Jean persisted, and eventually said it was something she really enjoyed. "Don't be surprised if something you think is going to be easy and good turns out to be difficult," she advised.

For years afterward, Jean would occasionally get sad and weep about her son's suicide. Pain is a stranger to none of us, and we all need blue blankets of one sort or another at various times in our lives.

Janet B., whom I mentioned earlier, acknowledged that even several years after her brother's death she still grieved and sometimes felt irrational guilt about her brother. "He was a very gentle person, even as a child. He was afraid of moths and I used to catch them and toss them in his face. Sometimes I wonder, and I know it's silly, but I wonder if that could have contributed to his taking his life," she said.

Letting go

Janet's reaction is not unusual. With any type of death of a loved one, we think of them occasionally throughout our lives. A song may bring back memories, or a certain food, or even an aroma can bring those loved ones to conscious thought.

Sometimes, though, survivors don't get on with life. The thought of the deceased is constant. Bereavement can offer a number of phases. Even though the experience is unique to each individual, there are commonalities. When the experience is delayed, though, when the stages are bypassed, or a feeling of hopelessness lingers long after the initial phases should have been experienced, it's considered a "complicated grief reaction."

Some studies show that people experiencing complicated grief are more prone to thoughts of suicide themselves.[12]

Although little is known about why some people fail to work through the initial stages of grief, some studies show that ritual helps, and when there are no rituals associated with the bereavement, it may make it more difficult to lay things to rest.[13]

Native Americans in the United States, beset with historic unresolved grief because of being uprooted from their former way of life, are finding that reestablishing those rituals can help to curb the fallout of that unresolved grief, which includes high rates of suicide, in addition to other social problems.[14]

Suicide expert Dr. Mamoru Iga, a specialist in Japanese culture, says the Japanese think any death is natural. "To them, suicide is bad, but they don't take it so hard. Americans have an unenlightened view of death and should learn to get on with life," he says.

"Japanese don't have the conception of hell. They have the family altar, the Butsudan, where remaining family members communicate with the dead. They can ask help from the suicide victim. Americans are afraid of death because they lose complete communication, but not the Japanese," says Iga.

Because many Japanese are, in a sense, in touch with their ancestors, they handle their grief by talking to them about why the person committed suicide. And they share their feelings of how it affected them. "They speak to them with love," says Iga. "This allows them to settle accounts with the deceased and to get on with their own lives."

Western culture, in the past few years, has adopted some of these methods.

Cerney used a method similar to Eastern tradition in dealing with grieving parents. Working with the process called "imaging," in which patients relax and envision the real past event or an imagined scene in their minds, she encouraged them to "image" the deceased and to speak with them. "I continually emphasize for them not to put words into the person's mouth. I believe the grieving person really knows the answers, but this helps bring it out.

"If they feel they have done something wrong to contribute to the person's suicide, they ask the deceased to forgive them. But first we must get rid of the anger. They are usually angry that the person could cop out on life—like a wife who is left with the burden and little income. We have to get them to accept or understand the person and why he or she did it, and they have to forgive him or her. The big issue is letting go. Then they are on a different level—acceptance.

"The survivors have limitations. They can't be responsible for others all the time. Maybe they did make some mistakes," she said, "but they shouldn't feel responsible for their loved one's suicide. One of the biggest problems is that they don't get social support because suicide isn't acceptable," she said.

Success of the therapy depends on how long they have been grieving and how much knowledge they have about suicide, according to Cerney. Therapy usually involves two or three sessions after being referred to her by their regular therapists.

"Some have been grieving for 20 or 30 years, and they all wish they had come sooner. Sometimes it's easier with long-term grievers. By that time, they've had other losses, and they know what loss is. But this isn't quick magic. It depends on the individual.

Some people can't use it. Those who use [the suicide] as a badge of courage, and have lived their lives as a martyr, don't really want to get over it. Their lives revolve around the grieving. But if people want to get over it and get on with life, they will."

In developing her methods, Cerney listened to her patients. When she asked them to use imagery to return to the origin of the difficulty that had brought them into treatment, they would frequently return to unfinished business connected with a loss. Other patients seemed unable to pass through the mourning process and get on with their lives.

"Perhaps imagery's main contribution in grief work is that it allows the individual an opportunity to handle unfinished business with the deceased," said Cerney. "Feelings not expressed before can now be expressed, misunderstandings can be clarified, and memories can be healed. Some patients, however, can't let go because the deceased has become an integral part of their sense of self. For them to let go would mean a loss of identity, a disintegration of the self. On some occasions, when I think the patient has worked through all the necessary issues, but the deceased individual still has not left, I may ask the patient what would permit them to let go."

Following the letting go, patients report a sense of lightness and freedom, said Cerney. "They are very tired, as though they have let go of a very heavy burden," she said.

Many people are able to work through their grief without professional help, but none need be ashamed or feel guilt if they need help in letting go of the burden.

Edwin Shneidman, noted suicide expert, wrote in *Suicide and Life-Threatening Behavior*, "With humans... this grief process... takes about a year. But, of course, the figurative sands of secondary grief stay on the beaches of our psyches all the remainder of our lives."[15]

Chapter 2

Survivors Speak Out

The mountain community in which I live is a resort and ski area. Frequently I meet people who are visiting, especially when I take my morning walks on the path around the lake. Over the years I've made a few friends with whom I stay in touch after they return to their own habitats, often in other states.

One out-of-state friend was interested in the book I was working on when we met. One morning when we met on the trail, she mentioned that her mother had committed suicide. Another morning she said, "Well, my mother was an alcoholic, and that probably contributed to her death by suicide."

When she returned to her own home we stayed in touch by e-mail, and I asked if she would talk to me about her mother's death. She said that the only thing she could say was to encourage people to get help, counseling, right away when a loved one commits suicide.

"These people are gone. You may think you don't need help, and that you are fine. But you're not. Don't try to be strong.

I didn't go for help, but I think it would have made a big difference all of these years, especially when I was going through the whole thing. It's still difficult for me to discuss. As I look back, and I think a lot about it, I would have done things differently. Maybe I still wouldn't have some bags in the closet if I had handled it differently. I know now that it's a sign of strength when a person can go for help. It's not a weak thing at all."

A daughter relives her father's suicide

"I can remember that day like it was yesterday," says Laurie S., a 35-year-old mother of two. "From morning to night. I can even remember where we had dinner. I was in college then. I was going to be a nurse. I dropped out of school when this happened.

"When I came home for lunch, I noticed that the car normally parked in the garage was parked in the driveway. I thought that was weird but didn't investigate. Later I found out that he had moved the van out and put his car in the garage. So when I was at home eating lunch he was in the garage. He was probably already dead. But I still have a little bit of guilt. It's still something in the back of my mind that says I should have checked into it. At first, I thought, what did I do? Why did we drive him to do this? It's so hard."

Laurie went back to school that day after lunch, not yet realizing what had taken place. After school, she went to her boyfriend's house where her best friend called telling her to get home, that her father had died.

Laurie assumed that he had died of a heart attack, as he'd had bypass surgery three years before and had been struggling to watch his diet and give up drinking and cigarettes.

"I just threw down the phone and cried and cried, thinking he had a heart attack. I cried the whole way home. When I got there everyone was in the living room. The coroner had already come and taken him away, because they had been trying to get me for a long time. So everyone was just sitting in the living room."

When Laurie asked if he'd died of a heart attack, they said no.

"I was so mad. So mad at him. Killed himself in the garage. Put the vacuum on the exhaust. No note. He got in the garage when I left that day."

Laurie recalls that an empty bottle of liquor was found on the car seat. "It was probably to help give him the courage to do it," she says. Her mom, who only drank occasionally, never touched another drink from that day forward.

She talks about how, at the time, she never realized how depressed her dad had been, and that he probably was depressed well before he had his heart attack. "I had no idea he was depressed. But I know he liked to drink. When we went to friends' houses, he always had a highball. He could make his drink whistle by running his finger around the rim of the glass."

Through the years, Laurie started remembering other things. About how quiet the house was. How her father stayed mostly to himself. How her mother and father never argued. Looking back, she sees that she never brought her friends home because they weren't really welcome. The house was quiet because her dad was depressed most of the time. "He was sort of in his own little world. He would watch TV."

At the time, though, she and her brother and sister thought it was normal. "We thought everything was perfect. They had a sailboat. They went sailing. Maybe they had a good marriage. So I didn't think it was odd." Now that Laurie has her own home and family, she says, "When it gets that way in our house—quiet—I sort of start talking. It brings back weird feelings. I want my kids to bring their friends over and to be welcome in our house.

"Suicide is a sickness. People don't realize they can overcome it. They don't get help," Laurie says. "And it can start with depression."

She understands that now, but at the time, she says, "I had problems talking to people about it. If anyone asked me about my father, I would think, 'Please, please don't ask me how he died.' I don't know if I was ashamed or if I just didn't want to go there. And if they did ask how he died, I would just say that he was a sick man.

"We still don't talk about it—sister or mom. He's just gone. It's a shame. I feel like my memories are being erased. It's like my memories are dimming. Or I don't know if they just don't want to talk about it. It's never brought up."

Laurie has a few friends who have also had a suicide in the family. They never discuss it.

"The other thing that was in my head all those years was that the church would turn its back on suicide victims. That they would blame them. That it might be a sin." She realizes now that most religious bodies recognize that suicide is mostly caused by a chemical imbalance in the brain, and that the person isn't responsible. Still, it's tough for her to talk about it.

And she still asks, "How many years did he contemplate this? Was he waiting until we all finished school? I was the youngest, and I had just graduated. Who knows? He could have been waiting, and waiting. Maybe he didn't want to burden my mother with raising all of us.

"When he died there were only two grandchildren and now there are seven, and he's missed out on so much.

"I never thought about it until I had my own depression. But I would never have the guts to do that. I thought my depression was awful, but the doctor told me it was a really, really mild case, but it made me think, 'Gosh, what did my dad's depression feel like?'"

A mother's story

As a former pediatric nurse and nursing instructor at Kaiser Permanente Hospital in Redwood City, California, Yvonne (Taffy) Hoffman had seen her share of dying children. She had comforted parents in their grief, but nothing prepared her for the suffering she experienced when her son committed suicide.

"You deal with a lot of guilt and anger. I have the feeling that when I walk into a room people are saying, 'That's the mom of the boy who committed suicide.'"

And anger nearly overwhelmed her when a well-meaning friend said, "At least you have four other children."

"I want to tell them that if I lost one of my fingers I'd want it back. That I lost a child and I want him back."

She lives with her husband, Saul, a mechanical engineer, and raised five children, including Dean, who killed himself by jumping off a cliff.

Taffy recalled that she was especially angry at the psychologists who had treated Dean, and who had failed to recognize the depth of his depression. And she became angry at friends who couldn't handle it—who shied away. "Once they just come forward and acknowledge and say they couldn't handle it, I'll feel better. Why do you suppose they shy away? I really think they don't know what to say. Part of it is that I don't have the energy to support them. It's really hard for them, I know."

But there have been friends who were especially comforting and still are. "At first, our closest friends were here with us, and they were helpful in that they just listened." People would call and say, "We were just thinking of you," and "How are you feeling?"

The pain is intensified when she reads an article like one in a major publication about four kids in New Jersey who committed suicide. "It [the magazine] referred to them as losers on drugs. I get upset, too, when I read articles that try to place blame when a young person commits suicide, such as, 'He/she did it because of lousy grades, or a breakup with a girlfriend or boyfriend.' What's that got to do with anything? There aren't simple reasons like that for someone committing suicide."

Taffy worried about her other children and the pain they were feeling. She said that after Dean's death at times they all climbed into bed together to hold one another like they used to when they were little.

Her husband, whom she described as a former "macho man," learned to weep and acknowledge pain and fear. "He's completely changed. He's much more into himself. He still gets uptight at different things, but reminds himself to calm down.

"Men don't have as many close friends as women. They don't have the support systems, but he's got one good friend who asks him 'How you doing?' and he knows he doesn't have to lie to him. He doesn't have to say, 'I'm feeling fine.'

"We game play. Each member of the family tries to protect the other. If I'm down, someone else tries to be up. Now we can acknowledge when we're down and that's okay. It's natural to game play, but it's important to be honest."

Taffy joined a support group, and the family received some group counseling. One particular counselor, who also lost a son, was very helpful, she said. One of her sons joined another support group, Survivors of Suicide, and rode a 200-mile bike-a-thon to raise money for a scholarship fund established in Dean's memory. Another son put his feelings into poetry. She and her husband helped each other through their mood swings, and they've stayed active in local youth organizations.

She said that she lacked energy the first few weeks after the tragedy. "Our rabbi made most of the arrangements. He helped us think. We could barely walk from room to room."

Nearly 300 people attended the funeral, and a little bit of tradition was broken. "One of the Conservative Jewish traditions is for each member of the family to shovel dirt into the grave site. Nearly everyone, including friends, took a turn and almost filled up the grave.

"It's powerful—the dirt. You are putting dirt over your own child. Life will never be the same, but then, life goes on."

When new acquaintances ask how many children she has, Taffy usually answers, "Five."

"Then it gets harder when they ask what they're doing, and I go 'uh...' and then I have to tell them about Dean.

"Another interesting thing is when you start feeling good. You're almost frightened of it. It's the guilt. You start thinking, 'Oh my God, it's my son and I'm not feeling bad.' You're damned if you do, and damned if you don't.

"Just don't say it was God's will. None of this was God's will."

A wife's perspective

Six months after her husband Richard's suicide, Diane C. struggled to put her life back together.

"It's just too big. I don't know any other word to describe it. Everyone has problems and you can talk them through and work them through and find solutions. There is no solution to death. It is so final. I mean, I can't ever go back. Can't ever recapture any moments. I don't have any control at all. I'm just powerless. I've never even had the word 'suicide' in my vocabulary. I never understood the pain Richard felt until this happened," she said.

"It's too bad it's just a complicated subject, suicide. The person isn't around to explain. My husband and I were on a 10-day cruise and we came back on Sunday, and I found him dead on Tuesday. We had one of the more intimate, wonderful times of our lives on the cruise...

"There were problems on the cruise, however. Richard, who was a psychologist, was recovering from the flu. He had missed two weeks of work, which was the only time in 10 years, except for one other day, that he had missed work.

"We had planned this cruise—I had just finished an M.B.A. program, and the cruise was a sort of motivation for me—and it was to be a kind of rehabilitation for him.

"He was still dealing with the flu virus on the cruise, and said he wanted to see the doctor. All of a sudden he was talking in terms of his depression, burnout, and overwork. It was obvious to us that he needed some intense therapy. We talked about it a lot on the cruise and decided he would see a psychiatrist, and perhaps, go to a psychiatric unit."

On the Monday morning following the end of the trip they went to the family doctor, and he suggested a psychiatrist, who then recommended intense therapy. Richard chose to enter a hospital, and he was scheduled to go there Tuesday.

"I left for work that morning and came home that night and found him dead. He chose not to go to the hospital. He must have decided Monday night not to go, because he left me a note that he'd apparently written Monday night. Sometime Tuesday morning he killed himself."

But Diane doesn't believe the suicide itself was something that happened overnight. "Now that it's over, I found a journal, and he had been having problems for a long time. It wasn't something like us having a fight. Suicide doesn't happen like that. People who are suicidal are suicidal for a long time, although I don't believe he decided to do it until that evening. It may have been out there as an option before, but I think having to come to terms with it, as a therapist, and with himself was the ultimate loss of control for him.

"Looking back I can see the signs of stress—the twitching in the eyes, his liver count was up, almost diabetic. Things were happening, and we laughed it off, because he was over 40. It wasn't until the cruise that we took it seriously. The doctor asked him if he was suicidal, and he told the doctor he had thought of jumping overboard.

"Of course, he [Richard] knew just what to say. He'd say, 'Yes, I had the thought, but I wouldn't act on it.' We all say things like that—'I wish I was dead'—but we don't act on it. But I became concerned about his emotional well-being on the cruise. The psychiatrist said there was no way to have known. 'I see suicidal people all the time, and I didn't diagnose him as really being that way,' he said.

"Richard wasn't psychotic. He was like anybody else who has depression. But it was much more extreme than he ever let us know."

Diane describes the night she found him as the worst in the world. "I walked in and he was lying on the floor at the foot of the bed facing the opposite direction. I ran up to him, felt his leg, and it was cold. I ran to the neighbors and they called the paramedics. They didn't try to save him. Rigor mortis had already set in. I called my family doctor, and the paramedics called my sister."

The sister came immediately, but the rest of her family, and Richard's, were out of state and came later.

She doesn't remember much more of what happened, except that she first called at about 8 p.m. The paramedics and the police did not leave until about 11:30 p.m., right after the body was removed. "It was horrible.

"Thank God I had a church. My religious background was helpful," Diane said. The minister who had married them, and who was a good friend, was with her the next day. For about 15 years, Richard had been playing poker with a group of graduates from the theological seminary he attended. The minister was part of that group.

"It really hurt those guys that Richard wasn't alive to confide or share with them," she said.

Diane returned to work after two weeks, and believes she probably needed three weeks. "That first week I mostly cried at work. In some ways, I thought it was good to get back to work, in terms of distraction. But in many other ways it just seemed like everything was so insignificant in comparison to my tragedy. Still, it was either that or stay home alone. The family had to go back to work, and it would have been worse staying in the house by myself. I didn't have anywhere else to go. I couldn't travel."

On returning to work, she found that most people were understanding, but would try to distract her rather than deal with the suicide. "Some people couldn't acknowledge his dying. That was worse than the people who came in and said, 'It must be really difficult,' and who allowed me to talk about it.

"There was a need for people to understand that I was a good wife. That I wasn't a nagging wife. That I wasn't the reason he killed himself. There was a need to let others know we had a good marriage and our relationship had nothing to do with him killing himself. There is a stigma about suicide. People don't know that it's more nurturing and more caring for someone to talk about it than for them to come in and start talking about the weather or work. People don't understand. They can't unless it has happened to them."

Diane believes that unless a person has been faced with such adversity, he or she may not know how to talk to the bereaved.

"My boss had an aunt die after I went back to work, and I went into his office and let him know that if he just needed to talk I'd be there. I don't know if I would have been able to do that before Richard's death."

She joined a support group where she received the understanding she needed. "That's one of the things about support groups. I was able to validate some of my feelings—even some of the physical things I was going through.

"I was thirsty all the time. Didn't want to eat. Became dehydrated. I had diarrhea. And of course I had trouble sleeping. Shock causes things you have no control over.

"Just talking with and hearing from people who have gone through the same thing helped. You are caught off guard. I think people are always caught off guard with suicide. You're always asking, 'what if,' wondering what role you played. What if you had done this or that. There are just questions that will never be answered."

Several things particularly helped Diane in the support group. One was that the survivors read the letters left by the suicide victim. "I want to show my letter, but who else wants to read it? But people who have gone through this know. We talked about what their faces looked like. Or what their bodies felt like. It's unbelievable how interested they are in hearing other people's experiences. My letter was so long. He wrote 12 pages. It doesn't say much. It doesn't tell me why he killed himself, but it says good-bye. Most of the other letters were much more brief. But the similarity is that you can hear that they're in a lot of pain, and you can't understand why. He said he was really confused and mixed up, and the best thing for him to do was leave. It's hard to imagine that. There had to have been a chemical imbalance. I don't believe my husband was rational at the time he killed himself.

"There are so many forms of depression. What's difficult about Richard's letter is that he is so controlled. If he hadn't talked about killing himself [in the letter] you wouldn't have diagnosed him as suicidal. He was so articulate."

Diane recalled that many of the other letters dealt with money problems. "My husband thought he had money problems. He was obsessed with it, even though he had a very successful practice. But he couldn't ever make enough. He made [the problem] out [to be] bigger than it really was."

The group also shared pictures of their loved ones, and that helped, she said.

"It's just important for other people to validate you. A man at my church told me it would take three or four years to get over the worst grief, and that helped me. I keep thinking it's been almost six months, and I think I have to hurry. So he gave me hope that I'm progressing and that I'm not hopeless. But everyone has a different time frame. It's like once the funeral is over, the show's over.

"The most comfortable time is the first two weeks. People come and cry with you. They want to hold you. People are around. The first time I had to stay by myself it was horrible."

Other help came from Diane's therapist, whom she had been seeing prior to the suicide. "There are so many people who don't witness or don't acknowledge, or can't acknowledge the tragedy and the pain when they lose someone this close. It's almost hard for anyone to conceptualize. My therapist was good at saying, 'That must really hurt,' or 'This is the most painful thing you will go through in you life.'

"My therapist says I should get a tee-shirt that says, 'I'm still in pain.'

"It doesn't help for someone to say, 'Go out to dinner and you'll feel better.' But when people say they understand how bad it feels, that really helps.

"I want to believe that it is the worst I will ever go through. It's a tragedy because it has totally changed my life. I had a life and now I don't have any. My husband was my life. The other things I do—my work and my school—were only secondary."

A friend talked her into getting a dog, a Sealyham terrier. He took her to meet it, and she fell in love. "And it helped. I've never had a dog. He just saved my life. So many evenings I come home and I just live for this dog. It needs me, and I need something that needs me. He's a wonderful dog. I've transferred so much caring from Richard onto him. It's amazing how much I'm attached to it.

"You can't realize until you lose your spouse how many things you don't know about yourself. You don't realize how many things you do because of your partner. All of a sudden you don't know what kind of furniture you like, what you like to watch on TV, or even if you like TV. It's just a tragedy that somebody I fantasized retiring with and growing old with, I'm never going to see again. I'm going to look at a picture of him when I'm 60, and he'll still be 43."

Diane says she'd like to remarry someday. "I'm scared stiff of a relationship, but I know I want to get married again, and I think that's healthy. If people have a good marriage and lose that spouse, it's not unusual that they want to get married again. Still I feel like I might be carrying so much garbage with me, so I don't know.

"If I ever get through it and to the other side and have another life, and I believe in my heart I will, I'm going to do whatever I can to help any other woman. No one should have to go through this, but they will. I'm 35 and no 35-year-old woman should have to go through this. It's just too big of a tragedy.

"But who knows what I'm going to do. I know my life ahead is going to have a lot of changes—that I have to die and be reborn, that I'm not going to live the same life without Richard."

Loss of a mother and father

Leslie Elliott was a metaphysical counselor living in the mountain community of Wrightwood, California, who vividly recalled the suicides of his mother and father more than 30 years ago.

"My father committed suicide when I was 11 and my mother committed suicide just after I turned 18, and I want to tell you, first of all, every suicide is a horror story, every one of them. It means that a person has obviously come to a point where they can't see beyond a certain wall. They feel there is no reason to go on living. None of us were consulted about coming into life. We were just brought here. We were brought here out of forces we had no control over.

"I always feel there is enough love and beauty [in the world] to anesthetize the pain [in our lives], but for some there isn't," he said. "I've spent 40 years thinking about this. Suicide is the anesthetic for this god-awful life we go through, especially for sensitive people."

Leslie recalled that when his father committed suicide by hanging himself at his office during lunch hour, he never gave any signs. "He never talked about it. There was no expectation."

Friends he was staying with in Wrightwood, whom he had known since the age of 5, told him of the death, but not the circumstances. He found great strength from them through this first ordeal, and others that beset him throughout his life.

In the 1940s, when Leslie was a young child, Wrightwood was a gathering place for some of the most noted metaphysical teachers and practitioners in the United States. Leslie was introduced, he said, "to their very fine minds."

Among them were Aldous Huxley and Dr. K.E. Mullendorf, the first woman ordained under Ernest Holmes of the Science of Mind Church. It was Mullendorf who broke the news to him of his father's death.

"She asked me to come upstairs and the first thing she said was, 'How strong are you?' and I asked her, 'Why?' She said she had something very serious to tell me. 'Your father died today.'

"She didn't tell me how he died, so the first shock was the news of his death. Suddenly you don't breathe. Everything just comes to a screeching halt. Death is so final in the sense that you never see that person again. I was silent. Speechless. If I had known him to be sick or disturbed, or hospitalized, it might have helped form coping mechanisms for the finality."

Mullendorf and a rabbi conducted the funeral, and afterwards, Leslie discovered a letter his aunt had sent describing the details of his father's death.

"He was a pottery manufacturer with a large plant in Manhattan Beach, and he hung himself in the office during lunchtime. The staff found him. He'd been a World War I veteran and had been exposed to mustard gas. He apparently had a heart condition none of us knew anything about. In the letter, he said he was afraid he would be a burden to the family, but I think there was more to it. That was my introduction to suicide."

Leslie said that after his father's death, the family fell apart because the relatives had never liked his mother, and they blamed her.

"She just couldn't stand the loneliness and isolation she must have felt. She had moments of feeling responsible. You can't escape feelings of guilt whether it is imagined or justified. You carry it the rest of your life. You never get over the feeling that this person has rejected you. 'What did I do wrong?' you think.

"I'm sure I had no direct reason to feel this, but I did. The thing that is so ironic in this situation is that people would say to me, 'People who talk about it never do it. Those who don't talk are the ones who do it'—wrong, wrong, wrong! My father never talked about it, and my mother never stopped talking about it until she did it."

After the father's death, the mother tried to talk her young son into committing suicide with her.

"I lived with the feeling that at any moment we were going to die. She was full of melancholy and at one time told me that when I graduated from high school, she would do it. When we were all teary eyed at graduation, I had the impression when the principal put the diploma in my hand that it was my mother's death certificate. Finally one day I told her, 'I know you're miserable, but I'm curious enough to want to go on and see what's around the corner.' I knew by that time I could deal with whatever I had to deal with."

However, Leslie always realized he didn't come out of the experience unfazed.

"I realized early on that I might never have a meaningful relationship. The residual feelings of rejection and distrust had stayed with me. 'Are they going to do the same thing? Am I going to get attached and then be left again?'"

Leslie, who was schooled in psychology, said, "There's another thing you go through the rest of your life. You have terrible feelings of pity for these people, but you are also very angry at them for leaving and rejecting you. That's a terrible ambivalence, but the anger is normal and healthy."

Just before his mother committed suicide, she quit talking about it, and Leslie grew hopeful. "She was cheerful. We planned a trip. She felt very content. I thought she was coming out of it."

After graduation, Leslie was sent to Wrightwood for a vacation. The last time he saw his mother was when she took him to the bus stop. When he returned home at the appointed time, she was supposed to meet him at the same bus stop, but she never came.

"I got down to the Beverly Hotel bus station and that's where I usually called her, but there was no answer. I thought maybe she was out for a walk and I waited, but then my heart started pounding and I knew it was the time I had dreaded for seven years. So I took another bus and got off and started walking up hills to the house carrying my suitcase. Something told me, 'Be ready now.'"

As Leslie neared his home he noticed three days of newspapers lying on the lawn. He opened the door, smelled a terrific odor, and then noticed his mother's body by the oven.

Leslie called a neighbor and after that, "Everything became a blur. I remember cops, the fire department... it was like I was in a state of suspended animation. It was a scene all built out of wax. From that time forward, I've never believed much in life. Something in me died and I've never come out of it," he acknowledged.

When I asked Leslie what kept him going, and why and how he continued to help so many people, he said, "As far as I know, one thing stands out. These people have met an end to their suffering. I get very irate when I hear amateur counselors say, 'You're never given more of a burden than you can carry.' That's out and out bull. We're given horrible things. I look at life as a jungle war, but still have rose-colored glasses."

Other things that angered him were when people who believed in reincarnation would say, "without any sensitivity" he noted, that whoever commits suicide would have to come back and live all over again. He also believed that religious fundamentalists who "tell you you're going to burn in hell if you commit suicide" were not only wrong, but mean spirited.

"Can you imagine suffering through a loved one's death and then thinking they're going to have to come back and do all of that misery again? No human being has a right to impose that terrible pain of seeing people who couldn't cope in this terrible life end it."

Leslie believed that he was fortunate to have been introduced to metaphysical teaching, and to the loving friends he made along the way.

"Somewhere along the line, I could have taken a bottle of pills, but I feel there has been an investment made in me, and I should respect it.

"It takes more courage to live than to die. If we're here to go through this, we're obviously here to develop some kind of understanding and maybe pass it on to someone else. I came to a point in my life that I said, 'If I'm here, it's for a reason. I'm not interested in me. I'm interested in feeling good. If I can get a good night's sleep, good food, and a pleasant walk..."

During that interview, Leslie would gaze out the window of his cabin in the mountains where tall pines grow. Some were dropping their cones to the ground, and a blue jay pecked at one of them. Leslie smiled.

He turned back to me and recalled a time when he became utterly depressed, and was complaining to a woman he'd met who had been through the Holocaust. "She slapped me and said, 'I want you to remember this all your life. Suffering is normal.'"

About two years after I interviewed Leslie, who had become a good friend in the year or so I had known him before the interview, he killed himself. He took his life at exactly the same age as his mother had—54.

The community was stunned. He was beloved. He was buried quietly, and a few weeks later a service was held for him at the community center. It was overflowing with people of all ages. Some had come from great distances. Young people spoke of his kindness. Old people cried. I miss a friend whom I dearly loved to be with. For years afterwards I'd say, "Jeez, I'd like to go talk with Leslie."

Others felt the same. A woman, the friend who initially introduced me to Leslie, and who moved from the community to Arizona, would cry over the telephone about how she missed him and continually ask, "Why did he do it? He was so beloved."

A sister's life and death

Carol V., in her late forties, is a former reporter, now freelance writer, and newspaper columnist living in Nevada. Her sister, whom we'll call Meg, was 35 when she committed suicide, but she had been making attempts since the age of four. The year before she took her life, she had finally been diagnosed as manic-depressive.

The writing Carol sells to many magazines usually concerns people who have overcome great difficulties in life—their triumphs and tribulations. She also writes about intolerable living conditions in women's prisons, and was once responsible for the early release of an inmate who, through her efforts, was found to be innocent.

Carol believes her type of writing may inadvertently be a way of working out the grief of her sister's death. Many survivors are propelled into not only reaching out to help the community, but in taking up work that helps resolve their own conflicts.

When the sisters were in their 20s, Meg reminded Carol that even as a little girl she had thoughts of killing herself. "It was frightening to her and she didn't know why," Carol recalls.

"She thought the first episode occurred when she was about three, but I remember her being four. I'll never forget that day. I was the one who was three. I remember her hurting herself like that and I wondered why she wasn't crying.

"She said, 'Carol come here.' It was the first time she had ever asked me to help her with anything. She was never too involved with the family—always one step outside. So I went to the bathroom and she climbed on the toilet and got into the cabinet and she handed me down an old Band-Aid box. My dad would put his old razors in there. He changed and got a new one everyday. Some of them spilled out on the floor and my sister said, 'Never mind that,' when I bent down to pick them up. We went back to the bedroom, and she asked if I wanted some and I didn't know what to say. I just got back into bed. She very methodically and slowly took one blade after another and cut her right arm and then her left, and she laid back and watched the blood trickle down the sheet. We were very quiet and she had a vacant look on her face.

"The next thing I remember was mother screaming, 'Oh, my God. What are you doing?' They were superficial cuts and mother cleaned it all up—ripped the sheets off. She was frantic. She didn't call anyone. She took cold towels and wrapped them around Meg's arms. After that, I don't remember what we did.

"The next time she acted out she was eight years old and I was seven. We had moved again. Dad was it the army, and we had moved around with him, and sometimes he'd go overseas for two years and we'd stay home. This time we moved to Wisconsin, where my mother's parents lived. We moved in with them. My grandmother was dying of cancer. Mother also took care of her father, who was diabetic.

"We were walking to school, a new school, and my mother was holding my sister's hand and all of a sudden she pulled away and ran out in front of an old '54 or '55 Buick. It swerved to keep from hitting her. The man driving the car was shocked and my mother screamed, 'Meg, what are you doing?' and Meg just hung her head as if she had failed again. That look on her face was like a puppy dog who had been shamed. She always had those big, sad brown eyes, and she looked down and didn't say anything. The crossing guard came over to put her arms around Meg.

"Mother didn't seem to understand anything, but it seemed to me that whenever Meg was faced with a new experience, she acted out. That first time, when she was four, she was getting ready to start preschool. When she was eight she was starting a new school, and when she began high school, her problems began to manifest themselves again.

"She was basically a very shy, introverted person. The friends she did make were very close to her but she always seemed one step removed from what was going on. It was after her third suicide attempt at 14, when she took a bottle of aspirin, that Mom took her to a doctor and he recommended a psychologist. So Mom took her. He [the psychologist] never talked to any other members of the family, and every time he talked to my sister, she came out crying.

"Mother also took her to the Christian Science counselor, who didn't believe in any of these chemical imbalances. She basically worked with retarded kids and she believed my sister was 12 years old emotionally. She didn't do one thing for Meg, who was in a deep depression by then.

"Meg wasn't bathing or washing her hair and she looked terrible. This counselor would say, 'I don't want you coming back here anymore until you wash your hair and until your appearance is better.'"

Carol says she hated the woman who was treating Meg.

"Meg was aware that she was different—that she didn't fit in. She talked a lot about dying. It was like she didn't want to have been born. She didn't want to be in this world with this illness she had. If somebody early on had said, 'Meg, you were born with this chemical imbalance,' and had the illness been explained to her, I think she could have dealt with it."

Meg wasn't truly diagnosed and given medication until about a year before she killed herself. During those intervening years, she dated, eventually married, and had two children.

Also during those years, the family disintegrated. "Mom didn't even want to be home. Dad was chronically depressed but hid it by just sitting and watching TV.

"I remember feeling helpless. Here was my sister in desperate need of love—of someone to put their arms around her and say, 'We're going to find out what this is and beat this thing together.' Knowing there was no help for her and probably never would be, it seemed like I was a child myself watching another child being victimized by her illness and her environment.

"Later we discovered that my father had a brother who was a paranoid schizophrenic. No one ever saw or spoke about his mental illness in those days. It was covered up. Even my dad was ashamed of his own illness. He also had a sister who was agoraphobic and became an alcoholic.

"By the time my sister was 18, everybody recognized that she had these real lows and highs. She married when she was 22, and I remember she didn't want to marry. He was our next-door neighbor. They got engaged at Christmas and she came up to the bedroom and said, 'I don't love him. It won't work out. But you know how Mom is.'"

Carol recalled that her sister tried to tell her mother how she really felt about getting married, but that her mother panicked. "Mom just wanted her out of her hair. She wanted to wash her hands of it. That was my impression.

"Meg's future husband was studying to be a psychologist and Mom felt that if she married him, it would help her. The marriage was rocky from the start, and grew worse through the years.

"I had to move away. I got to the point I could no longer live with my parents and around my sister. I loved my sister, but it was like being on a pier and standing by watching someone drown. I had gotten to the point where I ate my meals in the bedroom."

Eventually Carol moved out of state, but stayed in contact with her family and visited from time to time.

"Meg always talked about how all our lives she wished our parents would show some love. My father gave her a Raggedy Ann doll once—the only thing he ever gave her.

"She kept it on her bed even after she got married. On the morning of her death it was lying there looking down at her. She had taken a bottle of medication given for manic depression. She drank the bottle, laid down on the bed, Bible opened to the 23rd Psalm, folded her hands in prayer, and died."

Her young sons found the body and recounted to Carol that their mother's eyes were open, one staring at the ceiling. The head was twisted and the mouth distorted. "It was a horrible sight for her little boys, but it shows you how the body will fight to live. The body doesn't die easily."

Before Meg's final suicide attempt (there had been others throughout her marriage), Carol had visited her, and recalls Meg saying, "I don't want to die. I don't want to kill myself. But my thoughts get interrupted. It's just that with this illness I have, it makes me think I want to die. I can't think clearly."

Carol is glad that her sister at least understood that it was the illness that made her act irrationally. In a sense, it gave her some feeling of self-worth.

"When Meg died, my mother said an interesting thing. She said, 'It took a lot of guts for Meg to kill herself.' It bothered me because I wanted to say, 'No, it takes a lot of guts to live.' But in a way, Meg sacrificed herself so her family could get on with living and wouldn't have to be bothered with her. She knew that society couldn't deal with it—that her family couldn't deal with it."

Carol had a lot of bitterness about how her sister's mental illness was ignored. "The reality is, you're better off dead in this society," she said. "It's better to be born with a deformity that can be seen. It's worse to be born with a mental illness that no one can see. People want to bury it. They don't want to deal with it."

Carol acknowledged that she had to outgrow a lot of anger concerning her childhood and early adult life.

"I don't feel that way now because I have love around me. I had become emotionally cold. I set goals for myself, and it took me a long time to achieve them. That's why I try to be so good to my friends and to do special things for my husband and children."

But getting over her own feelings of inadequacy in dealing with her sister took a long time to resolve. Now that her own children are grown and in college that stress is gone, and she has a different, if still uneasy, attitude about her sister's suicide.

"When I last talked to my sister before her suicide, I was pregnant and not real healthy at the time. My marriage was breaking up, I had a 2-year-old to take care of, a full-time job as a reporter (very stressful job at the time), and when my sister called one day and started talking about suicide (like she had done so many times before), I said I couldn't talk to her about it. I had no energy to sit and listen to her problems. A few months later she took her life. That I regret more than anything. All my life up until then I listened and was like a cheerleader of life for her, but at that particular time I couldn't do it. I just couldn't listen to her heartache and give her a few moments of my time. I didn't have the energy and was too consumed with keeping myself calm and in a good frame of mind for the child I was carrying. Fortunately, my baby girl was born healthy and well. And today both children are off at college and enjoying their life. I wish my sister was here to see it and to enjoy how well her [own] boys turned out. But that's water over the dam."

Carol's mother died at age 66 of cancer. Her father eventually moved in with Carol, and they built an addition on to their home. Carol made peace with him, partly by coming to understand the illness that affected him. She says it's wonderful for her that she did, that her life is much better for making that peace.

Parents give and receive support

Jonathan, the son of Ira and Jeanne Jacoves, was described by his father as a "happy-go-lucky pro tennis player."

"If there are tell-tale signs, then people who are close can find the problem and get help for them, but it doesn't always help. They commit suicide anyway," said Ira.

Four months prior to his death, the family noticed changes in their son, saw his signs of distress, and contacted a psychologist. Jonathan began therapy, and was in and out of hospitals during those four months. Nothing helped. Just after his last release from the hospital, he killed himself.

"It's very difficult to accept and live with. You have a lot of self-doubts and it takes time to heal. Nothing anybody did helped, except meeting with other survivors. Nothing else was more satisfying than knowing others had gone through, and were going through, the same thing," said Ira.

Because of the help the couple received through support groups, they established the Jonathan Jacoves Memorial, which helps fund support groups for survivors at the University of Judaism in Los Angeles.

Although the Jacoveses found the kind of support they were looking for through the groups, Ira was perplexed that more men didn't attend them.

"We were the only couple going. Sometimes the husbands won't go, but their wives were there. That's too bad. They need to help each other. If you don't try to understand the situation and the feelings you have, you can't understand your spouse's feelings. You have to understand your partner's problems in order to help.

"I think no matter how hard it is for the father, it's harder for a loving mother. The woman has a different relationship to the child, regardless of what the courts are now saying. The father can be close, but biologically there's a deeper imprint on the woman. I'm not saying it wasn't devastating for me, but I didn't carry that child for nine months," said Ira.

"Whether you're the father or the mother, it helps to talk about it. You just can't keep it in. I had friends who were compassionate and understanding, but for a while, at first, I didn't want to see anyone. I ended up changing some of my friends. My outlook changed and I found I didn't need superficial friends. You can tell when someone doesn't want to get involved. Some people would rather close it out. They would say, 'Well, it's over, so get it out of your system.' I wanted to hit them. You don't want to hear anything flippant at a time like that. You learn that you don't have that much control over your life, much less someone else's."

Jeanne said, "One of the stupidest things people can say is, 'Now you know at least he's at peace.' Jonathan was having problems, that's true. But I think you would rather have the loved one with you even if they are distressed so you could help do something about it."

"I have a friend, and her son had been distressed for a long time, and she felt relieved when it was finally over. But not for me. I always think I can fix it.

"One of the reasons we set up a survivors' group is that the very term 'prevention' sets in motion that it could have been prevented. If you keep hearing that suicides are all preventable, you start feeling that guilt and blame again," she said.

"Most of the parents we've dealt with are loving, caring people who had tried to get help for their loved ones once a problem had been recognized. Still, the person committed suicide. You can't do a lot of intervention when the child is 26 years old."

The couple believes their closeness, and their ability to work through the bereavement together, helped, and they are fortunate for this. Too often, couples are torn apart when tragedy strikes a family.

Turning grief into action

Following the suicide of her 21-year-old stepdaughter, Lynn, Adina Wrobleski joined the American Association of Suicidology and attended their first national convention. The group was made up of professionals in the field, and Adina was the only survivor there. She says that they were not particularly interested in her perspective.

Four years later, however, she began researching suicide and its aftermath in depth, in order to answer some of her own nagging questions. Because her research was so extensive, and because she was approaching the problem as a survivor, she began receiving international attention, and attended the International Symposium on Bereavement in Society in Jerusalem. At that symposium, she presented one of her research papers on survivors, which was selected for publication in the *Israel Journal of Psychiatry.*

"It was the first paper done by an experiential person. There had been some papers done by the professionals on survivors, but they pictured it as pathological, dark, gloomy, and predicted pathological results. Up to that time studies of survivors had been conducted only on clinical patients who had psychiatric disorders or pathological grief reactions, and they had extrapolated from that.

"Up until that time, it was commonly believed that suicide survivors didn't get over their grief, and all needed professional help," she said.

Adina, however, based her studies on ordinary people— ordinary survivors—and found that the dire prediction of the professionals didn't hold up. "Based on my experience and that of others, it just wasn't so," she said.

"What I did was a maverick kind of thing. I didn't have a degree. But what I discovered is that if you have the knowledge you can establish yourself. The professionals accepted me."

When Lynn killed herself, Adina and her husband, Hank, "had been feeling particularly happy. It was just one of those happy something days. About six that evening the doorbell rang, and a police officer we knew as a friend was standing there.

"'I have bad news,' he said. 'Lynn is dead. She shot herself.'

"I can remember what must have been shock taking over my body. It was just like a huge iron door had slammed shut. You could feel the impact of it, but you couldn't hear it."

She remembered calling family and friends—"Just calling people over and over. It was sort of a period of being in a red kind of fog.

"The funeral period wasn't any different than what others go through, except people didn't seem to know what to say. I'd say to them, 'I don't care. I'm just glad you came.' I just needed to feel those strokes of love. Some people, virtual strangers, helped. There was a woman next door, a recluse. I hardly knew her and she brought chicken and cake over. I feel one of the good funeral customs is the bringing of food. I was incapable of preparing anything.

"After the first few weeks, we were by ourselves. That is the telling point—when everyone leaves."

That's when the reflections began. Adina thought about Lynn's earlier rebellions that had eventually culminated in a close relationship, especially after Lynn married. "That was the end of the pressure-cooker stage. After that, she kind of blossomed."

Lynn and her husband were getting ready to move into their dream house when she committed suicide.

"Things were going pretty good, and when she did commit suicide, I wasn't aware enough that other things were going on. There were warnings I didn't see. She obviously had depression."

Adina became aware of the darker side of Lynn's life only after her death, and after attending support groups. "It seemed clear that Lynn had depression since she was 9 or 10. The big thing nobody knew or recognized was that Lynn had abrupt changes of how she felt about the house that was being built. She began to fear the house. We went to lunch one day and I could see she was in a bad mood. We talked for four hours and I tried to reassure her about it. In the middle of that long conversation she laughed and said she'd had a gun to her head twice. I was so frightened I didn't know what to say or do.

"That just shows you how strong denial is. My experience now is that when suicide survivors are faced with this, the only recourse is denial. I felt helpless. I know now that I should have taken her to the hospital. So I am telling people to pay attention to these signs.

"Right in this great big restaurant she said, 'Thanks for caring about me.' I now think she was saying good-bye. But at the time I was puzzled and disturbed and told Hank about it when I got home.

"Anyway, the day after our conversation in the restaurant, she called three times and seemed confused. She'd say, 'Tell me again what it was you said yesterday.'

"Her last day she got up and got dressed. She didn't go to work. There are people who say you never know why people kill themselves. I know Lynn died because of depression, but the 'why' that haunts me is that moment she decided, 'Now is the time.'"

Adina believed that people do get over the suicide of a loved one, but that at the same time, the tragedy always stays with them.

"One of the things I'm against is the belief that suicide death is something you'll never get over, and that it will take years. The sense in which that is true is that it is such an awful thing. As you can see, I can go back there and relive the entire thing. However, I have this personal concept that inside a person is a little black pool of unhappiness where all the bad things that happen are put. Then I use the metaphor of a river, and coming back to walk on the ice on the river. Periodically we fall down into the black pool, but then we go on. As you get on through time you fall less far, and you don't fall as often.

"There is life after suicide. But we not only go through the grieving process that others do; we also have these extra things. You think if you had been kinder, better, loved more, listened more carefully, she wouldn't have died. This is the assumption you see in language. In no other death do people say, 'Oh, that poor family. They must feel terribly guilty.' We don't make this assumption with other deaths."

But Adina was optimistic. "I think the stigma is lessening. We have control over it. There are things we can do to prevent suicide. We can start treating the mental illness that can result in suicide medically and psychologically. We can get rid of our old beliefs."

Her wish, and that of many others in the healing professions, is slowly taking place. But as long as populations deny that people need help when they are depressed, and they hear the words, "Get over it," "Come on, you can pull yourself together," and other well-meaning but sometimes deadly phrases, instead of, "Hey, let's go get some help," depression will continue to devastate the lives of those needing help, and their loved ones and friends.

Suicide will always be with us. But as these survivors who have told their stories know, life goes on.

Chapter 3

Suicide Myths

Existing side by side with enlightenment on suicide's causes, prevention, survivor healing, and effects on society are ignorance, intolerance, and judgmentalism.

Even though various faiths are among the enlightened, and suicidologists and other mental health professionals try to get the word out about the true causes of suicide and offer help to the survivors, as many myths exist about suicide as they do about mental disorders as a whole. These myths make it more difficult for survivors to heal from such a devastating loss.

We are at the dawn of understanding suicide. In the past 10 years, research on how the brain works, and the rapidly increased mapping of the human genome have given the health profession new tools to work with.

In the first large-scale demonstration of psychiatry that a specific treatment can prevent potential suicides, 28 separate reports involving more than 16,000 patients conclude that the suicide rate among those with bipolar (manic depressive) disorder is six to eight times lower for those being treated with the drug lithium. Considering that there are more than two-and-a-half-million people in the United States suffering from bipolar disorder, the potential for saving lives through drug treatment is great.

Even with new research worldwide, new understandings, increased prevention methods, and the availability of more bereavement groups, the myths continue to surface. Even conspiracy theories, such as those surrounding the suicide of Vincent Foster, the high-ranking White House lawyer during the Clinton administration who had previously been diagnosed with bipolar disorder, might be perpetuated and furthered in part because suicide flies in the face of mankind's deeply rooted struggle for survival.

Also, unless the suicide is a high-profile case, such as actor Richard Farnsworth or Admiral Jeremy M. Boorda, people don't realize just how frequently suicide and suicide attempts occur. In 2000, Farnsworth, at 80 years old, was the oldest actor ever nominated for an Academy Award. He had recently been diagnosed with cancer. Boorda, 56, the Navy's top officer, was allegedly distraught over a controversy about whether he had worn combat pins inappropriately.

R.D.T. Farmer, professor at Charing Cross and Westminster Medical School in London said, "There are many possible explanations for the fascination that we have with suicide, and for the romanticism that surrounds its portrayal in fine art, literature, and theater. Perhaps the most likely is that self-destruction is perceived as being so unnatural as to excite emotions such as fear, revulsion, and recrimination."[1]

We're all affected by suicide

Once when I was speaking to a college writing class, the subject of my book for suicide survivors came up. Once the topic was mentioned, electricity seemed to fill the room and the students never let me finish the writing presentation. They simply couldn't break away from the questions they had about suicide. As it turned out, of the 27 students there, all but two of them had recently been touched by suicide, either of friends, acquaintances, or close family members.

One woman asked for the phone number of any support groups in the community. Her sister-in-law had committed suicide over the weekend. She acknowledged that her first emotion was one of anger.

None in the room had ever heard that some researchers believe that a great percentage of young people's suicide might be caused by bipolar disorder, schizophrenia, or severe depression. Most believed that one person could cause another to commit suicide, and one man became quite angry and said, "Of course a person can tip another over the edge."

"Not unless that person is ready to be tipped," I countered.

The instructor of the class related a story about a friend whose son committed suicide and how the mother was able to let out her grief, but the father had kept it inside for six years and was still suffering. Another man in the class countered with, "The fact that the father is still grieving shows there was something wrong with the family."

The instructor responded with, "That's the type of prejudice we're trying to overcome."

My experience with the class was overwhelming, and I was surprised by the hostility of some of the students regarding new research and thinking about suicide. Many still seemed determined to place blame. One man said vehemently, "It just has to be someone's fault."

When the class finally broke up (far past the allotted time), one woman showed me a list of names she had written down during the discussion. "Here are the names of six people I've known who have committed suicide in the past few years," she said.

Another class member, Mary Ortega, later sent me a story she had written about her grandmother's death. I'm sharing it here because it illustrates what may, perhaps, be the biggest myth of all—that somehow, some way, someone other than the suicide victim is responsible for the death.

My grandmother had been ill with some seemingly undiagnosed disease when I was about eight years old. She had been bedridden but lucid for a period of at least a year. A week before her death she got out of bed and tried to do housework. The doctor said she was not physically able to even stand on her feet. She was operating on mental power alone. She insisted that she was a burden to my grandfather and he would be better off if she were dead.

On the morning of her death, Granddaddy, who slept in the same room, awoke about dawn. Seeing she was not in her bed, he became alarmed and started looking for her. All the doors and windows were either locked or latched from the inside. He looked in the closets, under the beds, even in the cedar chest and kitchen cupboards. He couldn't find her.

Desperate, he called his son-in-law, Ialy, who lived nearby. Ialy disregarded all the places already searched and went directly to the screened-in back porch that housed two wells. One was quite large and contained an electric pump for the house plumbing. The top of this well was bolted down. A small portion of the porch had been walled up to make a room that encompassed the second well. This well was about three-and-a-half-feet high and was for emergency use in case the electricity went out.

My mother got the message by telephone. She was hysterical and could not understand why they were not using artificial respiration to revive her. Even after she was told the neck had been broken in the fall, she refused to believe that Granny was dead. Viewing the body made no impression on Mama. She kept repeating, "It's not true. She couldn't have done it. It's against our religion."

Mama blamed those that were present when the body was brought up because she thought they had not tried hard enough to revive Granny. My aunt and uncle, who were older than Mama, seemed to take it very well. My grandfather, on the other hand, was terribly guilt-ridden all the rest of his life. He blamed himself for not hearing her get out of bed and for the well not having a locked top.

Placing blame

Placing or accepting blame can become even more insidious than is related in Mary's story.

One volunteer at a suicide prevention hotline had received a call from a boy who had been badly beaten by the father of a girl who had committed suicide. The girl had left a suicide note placing blame on the boy.

The father's violent reaction was an attempt to transfer some of his own feelings of guilt onto another person, but since being blamed, the boy was contemplating suicide himself.

Although it is natural to want to blame someone, it is important for survivors to understand that no one is really at fault, although certain conditions that some people are forced to live under can result in the deep depression that can lead to suicide, such as a child or spouse who lives under abusive conditions.

Other severe types of trauma, such as those found in war-torn countries, devastation from natural disasters, imprisonment, and illness, can also lead to severe depression and suicide.

The myths

In the absence of open discussion and readily available information, people tend to form beliefs on the basis of sketchy news reports, hearsay, and offhand comments made by friends and relatives. What follows are some of the most current myths, some perpetuated by a kernel of truth that is taken out of proportion until it bears no resemblance to the truth.

These misconceptions not only hinder our knowledge about suicide, they thwart prevention and undermine the crucial support survivors need. As more information accumulates from ongoing research, complex issues behind the myths will become clearer, and society may begin the long process of truly understanding suicide and its aftermath.

Myth # 1

People who talk about (or threaten) suicide don't really mean it.

"Anyone who threatens suicide should be taken seriously. Approximately three-fourths of people who attempt suicide have given prior messages," said Alan L. Berman, executive director of the American Association of Suicidology in Washington, D.C.

The problem is, the signs they give aren't always clear until after the fact. "In retrospect survivors say, 'Aha, that's what it was all about.'"

Berman believes these messages are ignored for several reasons. "For the most part, what happens is that the message itself is anxiety provoking, so it is ignored as a defense against the anxiety."

In other words, family and friends try to avoid their own anxiety surrounding the potential of any suicide. "It goes against all instincts. The survival instinct is probably the most powerful, and when someone chooses to end his life before its time, it's very distressing to us," says Santa Monica private practice psychiatric social worker Sam Heilig, who also serves on the advisory board of the Suicide Prevention Center of Los Angeles at the DIDI Hirsch Community Mental Health Center. "A suicide makes us face the question about the meaning of our lives. Now what does that mean?"

Sometimes a person has threatened suicide over and over again until it becomes the story of "The Boy Who Cried Wolf," and is often ignored.

"What happens, however, is that the person, especially a youngster, is provoked into doing something more drastic. 'Aha, now I'll really do something,' the person thinks. Parents are often reluctant to get outside help. They feel blameworthy and they don't want to go public, so this adds to their guilt afterwards when the child attempts suicide," says Berman, adding that "It's different with adults. The signs [for teens] may be more subtle."

Bem P. Allen, professor of psychology at Western Illinois University, says, "Ignoring a person who talks about suicide isn't the best solution. Threatening suicide should always be taken seriously. It is a very important warning signal. There may be cases where that's all it is, but no one should make that assumption, even if it was just an attention getter. How do you ever know that?"

Also, there are instances where intervention doesn't help. One woman whose son killed himself at the age of 27, and who had frequently received counseling, had been trying to kill himself since the age of 5, according to his mother.

Heilig spoke of one woman in her 70s who had tried unsuccessfully to kill herself for more than 40 years. "There are simply people bent on ending their lives," he said, "and treatment isn't always successful."

Another story involves a young boy who had swallowed a razor at school, and had previously told three of his friends what he planned to do. He asked them not to tell anyone. He told each of the boys separately, and each thought he was the only one the boy had confided in. The boy was taken to the hospital and survived, but it could have turned out differently, leaving the other boys in turmoil.

More recently, a 17-year-old Granada Hills, California youth shot himself to death in front of classmates, particularly one girl who had just gotten out of her car and was standing fairly close to him. She is now in therapy. A troubled, but bright and popular youth, the suicide victim had told friends the night before that he was going to commit suicide, but no one took him seriously or reported it.

The boy who swallowed the razor, the youth who shot himself, and the woman in her 70s who had been trying to commit suicide may not seem to have much in common, but they did. Each was a potential suicide, and every effort needed to be made to save their lives, and that included taking their warnings seriously.

I've known of people who respond to a suicide threat with anger, such as, "So go ahead and kill yourself," thinking that a "get tough" attitude will jar the person out of it. Such a statement is like playing Russian roulette.

Myth # 2

Suicides frequently occur out of the blue with no forewarning.

Suicides with no forewarning are extremely rare. However, it is easier to distinguish the warning signs in retrospect, especially if a person isn't familiar with them.

"Anything remotely asked about suicide shouldn't be ignored. The slightest sign shouldn't be overlooked," says Professor Allen. "On the other hand, slight signs, such as a question asked during or after a class in which suicide was discussed, would not be a reason for action. Generally, it is a matter of who showed the sign and how many other signs did he or she show. If one knows that a person who shows a sign has attempted suicide previously, one sign is enough for intervention. For people with no known history of suicidal ideation or attempts, at least a few signs may be needed before action is taken. It also depends on the sign. If a person says, 'I wonder why people commit suicide,' more information will be needed. If a person says, 'I've been planning my death,' immediate action is needed. On the other hand, nobody can read the future. You can't be absolutely certain, and that creates a sort of dilemma."

Many people feel an uneasiness talking about suicide and might be embarrassed to ask, "Are you thinking about killing yourself?" Saving a life must loom larger than any perceived embarrassment.

Eight critical risk factors for suicide in patients with major depression have been reported by the American Psychological Association.[2] They are:

1) the medical seriousness of previous suicide attempts
2) history of suicide attempts
3) acute suicidal ideation
4) severe hopelessness,
5) attraction to death
6) family history of suicide
7) acute overuse of alcohol
8) loss/separations.

Myth # 3

If a person has been depressed and seems to snap out of it, the danger is over.

The greatest danger may be when a person who has been showing some of the signs of suicide suddenly becomes calm and seemingly happy. It may be that the person feels a sense of relief at finally making up his or her mind to go through with the deed. Getting over a suicidal depression is not an overnight experience. It can take months of medication and therapy for the person to get back on track.

The incidence of depression-caused suicide is controversial. Some mental health professionals say most people who commit suicide are suffering severe depression, though others say the figure is much lower. Part of the controversy may lie simply in the definition of depression. Although not all suicidal people are severely depressed, most are in some sort of mental or emotional pain.

Myth # 4

You shouldn't confront and talk to a person whom you believe to be suicidal.

It's okay, and even preferable, to ask someone who is exhibiting suicidal symptoms: "Are you considering killing yourself?" or "Are you having thoughts of suicide?" Ignoring it is a greater risk. For one thing, some experts believe that most people are ambivalent about their wish to die.

When suicidal people choose someone to confide in, that person should listen attentively. Try to reassure them that the feelings they are experiencing are usually only temporary. Also, let them know that they are not "bad" or "stupid" for even thinking about suicide. If there is advice given, it needs to be encouragement to see a physician (a medical problem could be causing the suicidal mood) or a mental health professional. If they are reluctant to do so, volunteer to drive them. In the meantime, emphasize that there are ways other than suicide to solve problems, and help them to explore some of those options. Because a suicide threat need never be kept confidential, ask family members and friends for their assistance. It could also be suggested that the person see a clergyperson, a guidance counselor, or a teacher who might, in turn, suggest a mental health professional.

Even if a person isn't sure when certain comments or behaviors promote uneasiness, it is best to ask the person more questions about his or her feelings. It's risky to try to talk a person out of suicide. If it's suspected that he or she indeed has thoughts of suicide, professional help is needed immediately.

Taking a vow of secrecy when a potential suicide shares his or her feelings with someone is also a bad idea. Young people are most likely to be asked by someone to "keep it secret." Education in schools today, however, encourages students to contact an adult immediately.

Myth # 5

Those who commit suicide are insane.

"To say that someone who commits suicide is insane is a myth from a number of standpoints. Insane is a legal term. It means the person isn't legally responsible, so it's totally inappropriate. Not everyone who commits suicide is legally incompetent," says Allen.

The suicidal person clearly is not completely rational, and may not be responsible for his or her act, but this doesn't mean the person is "insane."

This is not to say that a mental disorder can't trigger a suicide. Robert Cancro, M.D., professor of psychiatry at the New York University Medical Center, said that many suicides among young people are the outcome of undiagnosed schizophrenic illness.

Schizophrenics tend to attempt suicide early in their illness, and schizophrenia tends to have an earlier onset than other mental disorders.

"It is not unusual to see schizophrenic breakdowns in those between the ages of 15 and 18. In fact, the bulk of such cases have broken down before the age of 25," said Cancro.

Alcohol and other drugs are frequently found in the blood of those who commit suicide. "So it serves as both a facilitator and as a reason for committing suicide. It just simply is used to provide the courage or to make it easier to carry out suicidal thoughts," Farberow says.

Violence, too, can precipitate suicide, because in a crisis the alternatives for violent people seem narrow. They can't imagine a future. There is a subgroup of people who commit suicide after murders, with an estimate that 8 percent of all suicides begin with a murder.

Myth # 6

Suicidal people want nothing more than to die.

Professionals who deal with suicide note that most people who attempt suicide don't really want to die.

"They want to end their pain."

"They see no light at the end of the tunnel."

" They lose all hope that it will ever get better."

"That suicidal persons want nothing more than to die is an awful myth. Suicide attempters say they don't want to die. They just want to get away from their terrible feelings," says professor of psychology Bem Allen.

"There are more cases of individuals who were suicidal and who don't commit suicide than those who are suicidal and go through with it. Sometimes after getting help, they are healthier and happier than ever before," Allen adds.

Many people who attempt suicide are thankful when they are rescued, especially young children who often don't realize the finality of death. This doesn't stop them from thinking about it, however.

The sister of a young man who committed suicide recalls the night before he committed suicide. He called and began talking about his problems. "I just didn't have time to listen. At the time I had so many problems of my own I didn't think I could handle any more," she recalls. "Now I have to live with that. If only I had taken the time to listen."

Myth # 7

Suicide runs in families.

Although there is no "suicide gene," certain sociological and biological factors, some of which may be genetic, can run in families, seeming to predispose them to suicide. Statistically, a person is nine times more likely to commit suicide if he or she comes from a family with a prior suicide. In addition to an inherited predisposition to depression or suicide, it provides a role model for other family members.

What *can* be genetic is a predisposition to certain diseases that may lend themselves to suicide, such as schizophrenia, bipolar disorder, obsessive compulsive disorder, and severe depression. For example, research shows that people with obsessive compulsive disorder (OCD) have less activity in the frontal lobes and/or low levels of the neurotransmitter serotonin in their brains. Disorders such as OCD, compulsive gambling, anorexia, and autism also tend to run in families, suggesting a possible genetic link.[3]

Schizophrenia, which affects 1 percent of the world's population, may be linked to genetics, according to a growing number of studies, including one of 15 years involving more than 100 families and 1,000 participants at Johns Hopkins Medical Institutions.[4]

Additionally, studies at Rush-Presbyterian-St. Luke's Medical Center in Illinois found that one-third of the teens between 15 and 19 had family histories of suicidal behavior, often going back several generations. More than half of the teens came from families with a history of depression, alcohol and drug addiction, schizophrenia, and antisocial behavior—all conditions linked to suicidal behaviors.[5]

On the other hand, the causes for suicide may vary with different age groups, although older suicides, in contrast to younger ones, have some personality traits that place them at higher risk late in life, according to a report from the National Institute of Mental Health (NIMH).

The 1997 NIMH report stated, "research has clearly demonstrated that almost all people who kill themselves have at least one diagnosable mental or substance abuse disorder."

Many survivors of suicide report that they feared they might take their own life following the suicide of a loved one. There are several reasons for this. The first is that suicide has been added to their frame of reference where previously, they may not have considered it. The second is that they may be genetically susceptible to depression or mental and/or emotional instability, and this can lead to suicidal thoughts. Finally, even if there is no initial physical predisposition toward depression, it is natural for them to be depressed about their loved one's suicide.

Clearly, there is much more research needed on this.

Myth # 8

Once a person is suicidal, he or she is suicidal forever.

It's estimated that in the United States alone there are more than 5 million people living today who have attempted suicide.

"The important thing to recognize is that for many people the suicidal thoughts are temporary states of mind, and the crisis will pass, especially if they get help," says Peck. The crisis sometimes passes if they don't get help, but it is more likely to return than if they receive counseling or are hospitalized.

One friend attempted suicide in a motel several miles from where she lived, following the break up of her marriage and loss of a job. Before going to the motel, she had mailed letters to friends with directions of what to do with her belongings and estate. The letters arrived the day she made her attempt, and we were able to track her down with the help of police, who found her on the floor of the motel in time to have her stomach pumped from the medications she had taken. She was then transferred to a psychiatric unit for several weeks.

Following that episode, and the help she received in therapy, she worked, played, volunteered, and lived a full life until her untimely death from a cancerous brain tumor years later. And she put up a valiant battle to overcome the cancer right up to her death. She wanted to live.

Myth # 9

People who try to kill themselves, but fail, won't try it again because of the shame.

Although most people who attempt suicide don't try it again, it's not because of shame that they don't. It's usually because of the counseling, medications, or both, that they receive, and sometimes from a renewed understanding and caring attitude of friends and family. The danger, though, of second and subsequent attempts can be very real for many others.

For some people, once they have attempted suicide, the next time becomes easier because they've crossed a major barrier. It's like getting up the courage to try something new that seems insurmountable and finding that it wasn't so difficult after all. For every five people who commit suicide, four have made previous attempts.

Another point to consider is that suicidal people who are hospitalized receive constant care and attention, something they may have been deprived of before the attempt. Once they are released from the hospital, intensive care and attention is taken from them, and they are left without the strong social support they had been receiving.

Farberow points out that in the late 1950s and early '60s it was found that when patients were discharged from the hospitals in great numbers due to the increasing use of psychotropic drugs, the suicide rate increased because they lacked the social, intimate support they had previously been getting.

Sometimes, but not typically, family members will grow closer following a suicide attempt. One widowed woman, whose daughter in her late 30s attempted suicide, did not get along with her daughter for years, especially after the daughter announced that she was lesbian. Following the suicide attempt, the mother joined Parents and Friends of Gays in order to come to terms with her daughter's choice. She made many friends, both parents and their children, and eventually reached out to other adult children whose parents wouldn't accept them. She and her daughter grew much closer throughout the ensuing years, and now, following the daughter's retirement, the daughter looks after her aging mother.

It isn't shame that keeps one from attempting suicide. It can be love and understanding, as well as medical and mental health intervention.

Myth # 10

All suicides leave a suicide note.

Fewer than one quarter of suicides leave notes, and they are usually garbled. Often the explanations given for the suicide aren't the true reasons—only what they believe to be true in their particular states of mind. Because not all suicides are the result of depression or mental illness, the results of someone acting on revenge can be devastating if a note is left blaming a particular person.

Edwin Shneidman, noted American expert on suicide, writes in *Voice of Death*, "In order to commit suicide, one cannot write a meaningful suicide note; conversely, if one could write a meaningful note, one would not have to commit suicide... Life is like a long letter and the suicide note is merely a postscript to it and cannot, by itself, be expected to carry the burden of substituting for the total document."[6]

Patterns to suicide notes do exist, however, even though the writing may be brief. The elderly frequently write of intolerable pain.[7] A 1998 study of notes collected by Hong Kong police showed many were written by women who were non-widows (death of a spouse often leads to suicide in the elderly); they had no history of previous suicide attempts or diagnosed mental illness, and they displayed religious beliefs. Suicide notes by young people tended to be longer and more emotional, begging for forgiveness. The elderly wrote shorter notes with little emotion and they contained specific instructions.[8]

In another study after the downturn in Japan's economy, an increasing number who left notes cited financial problems.[9]

A study of notes from Ireland showed differences in those written by people who had been depressed and those who weren't. The depressed were more likely to write of problems in developing attachments and communicating with others. The researchers believed that notes can help in developing prevention programs, as they provide clues to the person's thought patterns prior to the suicide.[10]

Myth # 11

TV portrayals of suicide increase suicide among teens.

In April of 2000, the National Alliance for the Mentally Ill (NAMI), along with 15 other national groups, protested in writing a broadcast of *Wonderland* on ABC that ended with a powerful suicide scene. They pointed out that the program didn't adhere to the media guidelines prepared by the Center for Disease Control (CDC) and the American Association of Suicidology (AAS), which purport that certain media presentations of suicide may contribute to some viewers' taking of their own lives.

The debate over whether or not television and other media portrayals do increase the instance of suicide, especially in teens, has been ongoing for several years.

The *New England Journal of Medicine* reported in 1986 that in the 1970s, teen suicide increased significantly following 38 nationally televised stories of suicide.[11]

At least 40 newer studies throughout the world demonstrate that television coverage of real-life suicides, as well as fictional portrayals, unless they are handled correctly, do increase the risk of suicide in certain people who watch the programs, according to Madelyn Gould, professor of psychiatry at Columbia University.

"It's not the stories or the coverage per se, but how the stories are portrayed," she says. "The advice is to go ahead and cover the event, but to show it as a mental health problem and a waste of a life rather than romanticizing it."

Gould said it would have been more responsible if the earliest reports on Vincent Foster had mentioned that he had already been diagnosed with a major depressive disorder long before he took his life.

Allen believes that although showing suicide on television may not play a direct role in increasing suicide, it may serve as an indirect role by desensitizing people to the act. "It's similar to the violence on television. It desensitizes people. It tends to trivialize suicide. It's no longer a big deal."

Controversy also exists on educational programs about suicide, some of which are presented in schools in efforts to thwart suicide. Many professionals believe that not providing education and not talking openly about suicide increases the risk. Shneidman has likened suicide education to AIDS education, noting that prevention is nearly impossible without it.

Myth # 12

Cluster suicides are on the increase.

Public concern has been growing since the 1970s concerning possible increases of suicide clusters among teens and young adults. The CDC in 1999 acknowledged that our understanding of what causes and what can prevent clusters is incomplete, and there is no evidence that clusters are either increasing or decreasing.

Even the definition of what a suicide cluster is draws controversy in some circles, as studies show both that suicide contagion is real, or dictated by other elements that might make it seem like a cluster of suicides has occurred.

A cluster has been defined as a group of suicides or suicide attempts, or both, that occur closer together in time and space than would normally be expected in a given community, generally set within three months of the first one.

Cluster suicides, however, are not related to cult suicides, such as the 1978 Jonestown, Guyana mass suicide led by Jim Jones's People's Temple; the 39 members of the Higher Source cult who committed suicide in Santa Fe, California in 1997; or the nearly 500 worshippers who locked themselves in a blazing church in Kanungu, Uganda in March, 2000.

Suicide clusters are far from new, and some attribute the current cluster concept to the mid-1770s, when a novel by Johann Wolfgang von Gothe recounted the desperate plight of Werther, a young man who was hopelessly in love with a married woman. It ended with him taking his own life. Werther's particular dress style was picked up by the youth of that generation, and the book was also thought to have contributed to several youth suicides.

To put cluster suicides in perspective, however, perhaps 200 young people have killed themselves in what could be termed cluster suicides, whereas more than 10,000 teens annually do it in singular fashion. Cluster suicides make news but singular events don't. Another point has been made by suicide experts: Alleged suicide clusters in wealthy communities receive far more press than those that might occur in less prestigious ones.

The study of cluster suicides is ongoing, with one at the New York State Psychiatric Institute by Gould. She is looking at whether cluster suicides are really as prevalent as the media make them out to be, and what some of the causes and traits of students who take part in them might be. The study examined 53 clusters involving 208 copycat victims. Three to 11 were in each cluster.[12]

Although some older research has shown that one contributing factor may be that teens are particularly vulnerable because they can't stand the thought of losing a confidant or best friend, Gould's research shows that many of the copycat suicides were not at all close to the original victim.

Myth # 13

Most suicides occur during the holidays.

Despite the message of "holiday blues" beamed across the media during the November/December holidays, suicides actually go down during this season. So does serious depression.

Research in several countries shows that suicides are down during most major holidays, including Christmas in Western countries. In the United States, though, New Year's Day, the Fourth of July, and Labor Day see increases. Suicide hotlines receive fewer calls during Christmas holidays, during the World Series, during special events such as the Olympics, and during major natural catastrophes.

Some health professionals believe that celebrations and rituals, no matter how insignificant they appear, are heavy with meaning, and keep people from slipping into deep depression, or even dying of natural causes. One study of women who were close to death showed that they hung on until after their birthdays.

"They [rituals and celebrations] provide roots and foster a deeper sense of purpose and meaning in our lives," says sociologist and psychologist Calfred Broderick, professor emeritus at the University of Southern California. "We should celebrate every chance we get because life is tough," he says.

But there may be other reasons that the seasons and holidays either bring on or deter depression and suicide. A study in Denmark of more than 32,000 suicides in a 25-year period found evidence of the "broken-promise effect" (things didn't get better as anticipated) for major public holidays. It's *after* the holidays that suicide goes up.[13] A Japanese study also showed that suicide was at its lowest before a holiday, and highest afterward.[14]

Myth # 14

Most suicides occur at nighttime.

Nighttime seems to be more mysterious and foreboding, but suicides occur at every hour of the day and night. And more suicides occur in the spring and late summer when daylight is extended. It is believed that the spring peak has reflected the hope of those who made it through the winter with its colder weather, shorter daylight hours, and isolation. They expect things to get better, and when they don't, they become depressed.

"Spring is a transition season, when things change very rapidly," observed the late Helmut Landsberg, a meteorologist at the University of Maryland. "This change in light seems to affect human glands and internal reactions."

In another twist, a Norwegian study revealed a distinct pattern of seasonal variation in the frequency of violence, including suicide, tied to latitude, with peaks in May through June and October through November. It could be that the abrupt changes from nearly 24 hours of daylight or darkness to the opposite create a general malaise in Northern latitudes. This is unlike the countries in mid-latitude, where the changes from light to dark aren't so dramatic.[15]

Michael Gauquelin, a French psychologist, writes in *How Atmospheric Conditions Affect Your Health,* that even without the dramatic shifts in light and darkness, "Spring is a period when new romances start, when fresh plans are made... but it is also a season when people experience frequent changes of mood and have bitter arguments with one another."[16]

Myth # 15

Women threaten suicide, but men go through with it.

It is true that more men than women kill themselves, but women do kill themselves. What doesn't appear to be true is that women don't really mean it when they attempt suicide.

Five to eight times as many men kill themselves, yet more women attempt suicide than men, and more women seek treatment for depression. Men are more successful at suicide partly because they use more violent, direct methods, such as shooting or hanging themselves. Women tend to try pills and carbon monoxide poisoning.

The methods are changing, though, with more women using guns than ever before. The change, according to some researchers, is because barbiturates, frequently used to commit suicide, have gotten more difficult to obtain, whereas it's easy to get a gun.

In addition to men using more violent methods to kill themselves, they also experience higher levels of alcohol and drug use, and are less likely to seek medical care to be treated for depression.[17] Also, more than 90 percent of homicide-suicide offenders are men. Frederic Rabinowitz, professor of psychology at the University of Redlands in California, and coauthor of *Men and Depression: Clinical and Empirical Perspectives,* asks, "How many men who are desperately depressed ultimately end their pain and shame in such a fashion?"[18]

Myth # 16

Celebrities are more prone to suicide than the general population.

Celebrities are no more likely to commit suicide than anyone else. It may seem they do, but that's because their names make headlines.

"It's the media that gives us the impression that they are more prone. For a long time, the media wouldn't print suicides, especially when it was a youth, but that has changed and it's good. Suicide needs to be made public so that others will be more aware of what is happening," says Allen.

Traditionally, newsrooms have had a policy of printing only the suicides of notables, or if the suicide took place in an unusual setting or circumstance. Sometimes the media cannot obtain information anyway, because most police departments won't release the names of suicide victims in efforts to protect the families, or to avoid lawsuits.

It may be that if celebrities talk about their own thoughts of suicide, or speak out when other notables take their own lives, they can help shatter some of the myths surrounding suicide.

They can let the public know that suicide isn't something to hide in the closet, and that a greater proportion of the population than we ever realized has considered it.

When someone like Sid Caesar acknowledged that he had thoughts of suicide, or when a seemingly gentle man like Iron Eyes Cody, cast as the crying Indian for environmental commercials, talked about his thoughts of suicide, it makes us realize that suicide is a stranger to no one.

Cody said that after his wife died he returned to his lonely Montana cabin and tried to commit suicide. He took some pills and lay by the lake in his sleeping bag thinking he would never wake up. That is, until some geese began biting him. Later, he tried to run his white Cadillac off a mountain road, but that too failed.

Rod Steiger is one of the latest celebrities to talk and to write about his deep depression. A few of the others include CBS TV news journalist Mike Wallace; baseball player Darryl Strawberry; political advisor and educator George Stephanopoulos; tennis star Monica Seles; actress Winona Ryder; musician Bonnie Raitt; Alma Powell, wife of the Secretary of State Colin Powell; former First Lady Barbara Bush; actor and comedian Jim Carrey; "Peanuts" comic strip author Charles Schultz; and musician and actress Dolly Parton. These celebrity acknowledgments, rather than signifying that they are more prone to depression and thoughts of suicide, may simply be a composite of the general population. Celebrities have a greater chance of being interviewed by the media, and may possess fewer inhibitions in talking about it. It is believed by many experts that when celebrities talk about their own disorders and the help they received, it encourages others to overcome the stigmas attached to mental disorders.

Myth # 17

Minorities in the United States are more prone to suicide.

The exact opposite is true. Blacks and most other minorities have one of the lowest suicide rates in the United States, although it has been increasing the past few years. Native Americans are the exceptions, with a suicide rate higher than the overall rate.

A black man being interviewed on TV once said, "Blacks don't commit suicide like the rest of the population because we've learned to live with the blues throughout our entire lives."

Comedian Dick Gregory once said, "You can't kill yourself by jumping out of the basement."

Richard J. Seiden, former professor of behavioral sciences at the University of California at Berkeley, says the rest of the population can learn from the coping style of blacks.

"I'm not saying people should live in poverty and suffer from discrimination, but it seems the people with most to live for, which is white males, have the hardest road. I have the feeling that one of the variables is how much you aspire to. I think a lot of people are very unhappy because of the standards they set for themselves. They are frustrated. We need to look at the coping skills developed by minorities to learn to adapt to these frustrations.

"I've found that in studies of students who kill themselves, one of the first hypotheses to be put forth is that they must be doing terrible in school, but it turned out to be the opposite. Students who kill themselves have all sorts of honors and higher grades, but have an internal feeling of not being happy with themselves," says Seiden.

Ironically, black college students and women of all races are becoming more like white males in terms of suicide. "It really isn't a racial difference in the genes. It is a class system. We find it all over the world. People in the upper classes all over have a higher suicide rate. Even studies done in the armed forces show that officers invariably have higher rates than enlisted men. As more blacks become involved in the American dream—that is, material success—their suicide rates increase," says Seiden.

Along with material success comes increased suicide rates among the elderly of various cultures as their children move towards their slice of the pie.

In non-industrialized countries, suicide rates among the old are extremely low. As countries become modernized and industrialized, they're no longer interested in the wisdom of the elders. Because the old are no longer valued, their suicide rates begin to increase. It's a matter of feeling useless, worn out, and isolated, according to Seiden. (Other factors, such as the pain of cancer or other illnesses, also contribute.)

"In minority communities there isn't enough money to hire help to take care of the children and to prepare all the meals, so the elderly are needed. In affluent families, they can hire help and send the old to homes," says Seiden.

Although the suicide rate among old people is higher in industrialized countries than for any other age group, it is declining in the United States. Seiden links this decline to the increased political power of the elderly. It gives them the idea that they can do something to change their lives and have more control over it. "Suicide comes from a feeling of helplessness that nothing can be done. That's how people think before they kill themselves."

Myth # 18

More poor and uneducated people commit suicide.

"It's a misconception that more bad things happen to poor people. Money has nothing to do with it," says Allen. "Suicides affect all strata of society and occur at all socioeconomic levels. Rich people who face loss of status or fortune can be as vulnerable as poor people who may find a continued struggle unendurable. There is no single type of suicide, suicidal person, or suicidal vulnerability."

Consider that the suicide rate of physicians and anesthesiologists is higher than for the general population in many countries.[19, 20, 21] Psychologist Michael Peck points out that college students who commit suicide tend to come from intact, middle-class families, and to be average students. They aren't neurotic, nor do they have problems with grades in school.

Javad H. Kashani, M.D., professor of psychiatry, says that one-fourth of college freshmen will consider suicide. Suicide is the second leading cause of death among college-aged people. He believes it is caused from the pressure of coming from childhood to young adulthood, and the pressure to do well academically. The stress leads to depression and is often accompanied by alcohol or drug abuse.[22]

Myth # 19

Religious people are less likely to commit suicide.

There are no specific laws in the Bible against suicide. It wasn't until the fifth century A.D. that laws were invoked by church leaders based on the commandment "Though shalt not kill."

People of all religious faiths commit suicide and always have, although they and their surviving families were treated far differently in the past than they are today, at least by most religious bodies. Because it is known that involvement with others offers some protection against the depression that can result from loneliness and alienation, the church may offer some protection against suicide.

"The degree to which one is religious, otherwise known as 'religiosity,' may protect one from suicide in that the attachment to an institution of religion (church, synagogue, etc.) and to the rituals and systems of religion can be significant to one's sense of self, of value, of purpose, and so forth. Some religions have higher versus lower rates of divorce among adherents, and marital status is an important demographic variable in our understanding of risk versus protection. However, no one religion seems to be immune from suicide, and some religions may promote a wish to join with God for some who are delusional," says Berman.

Chapter 4

Who Commits Suicide?

The World Health Organization (WHO) reports that in the last 45 years, suicide rates have increased 60 percent worldwide. Suicide is now among the three leading causes of death among those aged 15 to 44 (both sexes). According to the Surgeon General's 1999 "Call to Action to Prevent Suicide," there are an estimated four-and-a-half million suicide-attempt survivors nationwide.

Although suicide rates have traditionally been highest among elderly males, rates among young people have been increasing to such an extent that they are now the group at highest risk in a third of all countries, according to WHO.

Mental disorders, including depression, are associated with more than 90 percent of all cases of suicide worldwide. However, the conditions leading to the mental disorder and suicide result from many complex sociocultural factors and are more likely to occur when someone faces the loss of a loved one, a job, honor, a safe place to live, and under certain conditions of war, such as torture or incarceration.

WHO acknowledges that statistics on suicide are difficult to come by and may be inaccurate because of the sensitivity of the issue, particularly in countries where suicide is an absolute taboo, although it occurs, nonetheless, in keeping with the rest of the world.

The governments of many industrialized nations are making concerted efforts to lower the rates of depression and suicide, along with the stigma attached to mental disorders, because it impedes getting help for the victims.

The following suicide rates were supplied by WHO and are based on the most recent available percentage of suicides per hundred thousand population:

Australia	1997	14.7
Barbados	1995	06.5
Canada	1997	12.3
France	1995	20.6
Great Britain/Ireland	1997	07.1
Israel	1996	05.4
Mainland China	1987	10.0
Mexico	1996	03.1
Netherlands	1994	06.7
New Zealand	1997	14.0
Puerto Rico	1992	08.7
Russian Federation	1995	41.5
Singapore	1997	11.1
Sweden	1996	14.2
United States	1996	11.8
Yugoslavia	1996	15.3
Zimbabwe	1990	07.9

According to the Centers for Disease Control, more people in the United States die from suicide than homicide, and in 1997 there were one-and-a-half times as many suicides as homicides.

Overall, says the CDC, suicide is the eighth leading cause of death for all Americans, and it is the third leading cause of death for young people aged 15 to 24.

Even though females attempt suicide more frequently, males are four to eight times more likely to die from suicide because of the more lethal means used, such as guns or hanging, and their higher levels of alcohol and drug use.

We can't know what goes on in the deepest recesses of a person's mind. That's why suicides or suicide attempts of notables, such as artist Vincent van Gogh, poet Sylvia Plath, author Ernest Hemingway, actress Marilyn Monroe, author Virginia Woolf, actress Clara Blandick (who played Aunt Em in the Wizard of Oz), actress Drew Barrymore at age 13, and Elizabeth Wurtzel, author of *Prozac Nation,* intrigue us. Wurtzel acknowledges that she was clinically depressed at the time of her suicide attempt.

Certain groups are at higher risk

Other than a clear diagnosis of particular mental disorders, such as clinical depression, schizophrenia, or bipolar (manic depression), we seldom know what goes on in a person's life to trigger a deep enough depression to lead to suicide. Ongoing studies today, though, show high suicide rates for women who suffer spousal abuse; children who are abused; Vietnam vets; homosexuals; the elderly, especially men; teens; Native people in industrialized countries; and people who suffer debilitating and painful diseases. Police officers also have a high rate of suicide, and are three to eight times more likely to die by their own hand than from homicide.[1]

It's believed that exposure to violence, human misery, the promotional process, shift work, lack of control over their jobs, substance abuse, illness, and severe emotional problems account for police officers' high rates of suicide.

However, rates for veterinary surgeons, pharmacists, dentists, farmers, and doctors are also among the highest in suicide, partly because some of those occupations provide easy access to both the methods and knowledge of suicide. Also, these occupations may be particularly prone to stress and, in the case of farmers, to financial difficulties and isolation. Financial difficulties are a major stressor, with suicide increasing during the Great Depression of the 1930s. But it was not the tycoon who had lost huge sums of money jumping from the Empire State building who brought up the figures. It was the common family man, worried, depressed, and anxious over trying to feed his family. The late 1990s economic slump in Japan also increased suicides there.

Debilitating and painful disease is also a trigger, because depression becomes a factor in many of those cases, including some who opt for euthanasia. Cancer patients tend to become depressed or hopeless or both, which leads to a wish to die. Researchers are studying whether or not antidepressants can help cancer patients alleviate the wish to die.[2]

Some studies show that 35 to 40 percent of battered women in the United States attempt suicide.[3] Worldwide research shows similar or more stark statistics on abused women. One study in New Guinea showed that more than 50 percent of suicides attempted by women were precipitated by a beating by the woman's husband.[4]

The elderly

The elderly have one of the highest suicide rates in many industrialized countries, with older men at higher risk than women. Men over the age of 55 in the United States have six times the suicide rate of the national average, according to Steven E. Hyman, M.D., Director of the National Institute of Mental Health.

Also, 37 percent of those in primary care settings experience symptoms of depression, and when first arriving at a nursing facility more than 50 percent are depressed. But it is not just those who are in nursing facilities that bring up the rates of suicide for older people.

A study at the University of Oxford found that because drug overdoses are one of the prevalent methods of suicide, general practitioners need to improve the way analgesics and antidepressants are administered. A high proportion of the elderly at risk often consult their general practitioner prior to taking their own life. General practitioners, on the other hand, have a difficult time identifying those at risk because of the high proportion of physical complaints in the elderly that might obscure signs of depression.[5]

Hyman told the Senate Appropriations Committee Subcommittee on Labor, Health, and Human Services and Education in February, 2000 that, "More so than among other age groups, depression in the elderly is often obscured by symptoms of physical illness, and by loss and loneliness that all too often mar late life; thus depression is not recognized or treated adequately."

Adding to the dilemma are physicians who recognize depression, and the potential for suicide in middle-aged and older adults, but are less willing to treat them for the condition than younger patients. Studies find that many believe that being depressed and thinking about suicide is rational and normal in the aged.[6]

Yet, treating depression in the elderly can be effective, with studies showing that suicide is reduced when general practitioners are trained to deal with it.[7]

"The elderly are not more unhappy and are probably not more depressed than others, but they do get depressed and, of course, should receive treatment just like anyone else. These physicians are accepting the stereotype that depression is 'normal' for elderly people, and that is not true," says Bem P. Allen, professor of psychology at Western Illinois University.

As if in a vicious circle, some of the strongest evidence so far suggests that people who commonly experience symptoms of depression are more likely to develop heart disease.[8] Depressive symptoms aren't a cause of the disease, but might predict its development.

In a multicenter, six-year study of people age 65 or over who were initially free of heart disease, researchers from the

Cardiovascular Health Study Collaborative Research Group found that those who reported feeling symptoms of depression were 40 percent more likely to develop heart disease than those who reported feeling depressed the least often.

One of the greatest recognized contributors to suicide in the elderly, however, is bereavement over the loss of a spouse, especially among widowers.[9]

Ironically, bereavement symptoms of less than two months don't qualify as a mental disorder, even though it can be debilitating and can lead to severe depression, suicide, and some physical illnesses.

Risk for sexual orientation

Because a great deal of bigotry and prejudice still exists against the homosexual community, and because of problems of adapting and fitting in, especially in youth, their suicide rate remains high.

Studies from North America and New Zealand show that gay and bisexual males are at least four times more likely to report a serious suicide attempt than their non-gay counterparts.[10] Another study in Calgary, Canada, of males aged 18 to 27 years who were asked about sexual activity and orientation, classified 13 percent as homosexual and bisexual. They reported higher rates of previous suicidal ideas and attempts. The studies showed that homosexual and bisexual males were nearly 14 times more at risk for a serious suicide attempt than their heterosexual male counterparts.[11]

Researchers attribute the youthful homosexual community's high risk for suicide to a climate of hostility, which conditions them to hide their feelings from others or to risk "coming out" to family and peers, thus hindering any support they might need. With no one to talk to and no support, the youthful males, who experience plenty of problems just "growing up," get double-dosed with the problem of not understanding their own sexuality.

Although AIDS is not a disease that affects only homosexuals, the onset of AIDS has increased the incidence of suicide disproportionately in the homosexual community. New treatments, however, are offering more hope, and the rate of suicide for AIDS patients is expected to diminish.

However, older persons with AIDS continue to experience high rates of depression and thoughts of suicide, in part because they perceive that they receive less social support from family and friends.[12] Also, the friends of many older persons with AIDS may have already died, leaving less of a support system.

Studies also show that women who are both pregnant and HIV positive may be at particularly high risk of suicidal behavior.[13]

Teens and adolescents

While youth suicide in the United States has remained relatively stable since its high in the 1960s, it has more than doubled in Australia and New Zealand. Those countries are making concerted efforts to cut the rates, which are mostly linked to mental disorders and substance abuse.[14]

In line with the medical center's finding, the 1999 Mental Health: "A Report of the Surgeon General" said that "The incidence of suicide attempts reaches a peak during the mid-adolescent years, and mortality from suicide, which increases steadily through the teens, is the third leading cause of death at that age."

Several other factors can place teens and adolescents at greater risk for suicide. It's believed that teens and adults who suffer early-onset depression when they are younger are at higher risk for suicide.[15] Even with this finding, other studies show that teens are not likely to receive needed therapy.[16]

"It's a huge problem. Only about 25 percent of depressed teens receive help," says Paul Rohde, psychologist and research scientist at Oregon Research Institute. "One of the myths of suicide is that teens don't want to talk about their feelings of depression and thoughts of suicide if someone asks them. They are often very willing to talk about feelings of depression and thoughts of suicide if someone asks them."

Rohde says that of 65 identified depressed teens, only about 15 adolescents said their parents knew about it. The parents of 10 others said their teen was depressed, but the teen denied it. The other 40 teens said they were depressed, but their parents didn't know about it. Even when a teen has made a non-lethal suicide attempt, parents frequently don't know about or ever learn of it. One of the problems is that, unlike adult depression, teens don't always show symptoms of sadness or lethargy. Instead, they may show signs of irritability, or anger, and conflict with family members and peers.

Incarcerated youths are also highly vulnerable to suicide, especially if they don't have the support of parents.[17]

Traumatic grief can also instigate thoughts of suicide in teens, making them five times more vulnerable to thoughts of suicide.[18]

The possible reasons for increased risk of suicide in youth is endless. A study in 1985 headed by the late Dr. Lee Salk, a child and family authority, studied the backgrounds of people who committed suicide prior to their 20th birthdays. He found that their mothers had received less prenatal care and were more likely to have smoked and drunk alcohol during pregnancy than a control group. Some researchers believe that stress in the womb can lead to any number of mental disorders, including depression, linked to the fetus' changed brain chemistry.[19]

The 1999 Surgeon General's mental health report said that suicide reaches a peak during the mid-adolescent years, and that mortality from suicide increases steadily in the teen years, becoming the third leading cause of death at that age. The report also backed studies showing that more than 90 percent of children and adolescents who commit suicide have a mental disorder.

Some researchers and other mental health professionals believe that alcoholism among parents may be an even more important factor in youth suicide than alcohol abuse by young people themselves. Research in the past 20 years has clearly shown that children raised in alcoholic families suffer a host of problems even into old age, including depression.

Children

Suicide is the 10th leading cause of death in children aged one through 14 years old. For each child who commits the act of suicide, there are at least 50 more who attempt it. However, it is difficult to collect statistics on suicide in children due to the lack of standard criteria used to determine suicide in this age group, as well as the myths surrounding childhood suicides.[20]

One study found that nearly 10 percent of a group of school-children ages six to 12 had suicidal ideas. It is believed that these children, who already have thought of suicide, may develop self-destructive behaviors in adolescence and beyond. Some experts speculate that the reason so many young people attempt suicide in the evening hours is because someone will be around to save them. They don't really want to die.

"When we ask kids, 'Did you really mean to kill yourself?' they frequently answer, 'I don't know,'" says Richard T. Monahan of McLean Hospital and Harvard Medical School.

Michael L. Peck, a Santa Monica psychologist in private practice, says that most adolescents who are suicidal tell a friend. "They don't tell a teacher. They don't tell a counselor or parents. They tell a friend first, usually a classmate. We found that 25 to 30 percent of all 10th-grade students in a survey had had a friend tell them about a planned suicide. When you go into the classroom and ask for a show of hands on 'How many of you have had a friend tell you?' you'd be amazed. So the idea is to educate them as to what to do. How to handle it. How to know when their friends say not to tell anybody, that they don't pay any attention to that."

When a youth confides an intent to commit suicide to a friend, the friend should tell a school official or the parents. The parents then need to seek professional help for their child immediately.

Children of all ages, including infants, can experience depression. Depression among the young leading to suicide can be linked to hereditary factors, loss of a loved one before the age of 12, violence, decreased family ties, and increased family pressures.[21]

Children with learning disabilities experience higher levels of depression that can lead to suicide. A study at the University of Minnesota showed that adolescents with learning disabilities had twice the risk of emotional distress as those without disabilities, and that girls in that subgroup were at twice the risk of attempt-ing suicide as their peers.[22]

As could be expected, close ties with their parents and with the school diminished the children's emotional distress.

Also, men who were sexually abused as children have higher rates of borderline personality disorder, depression, and suicide attempts.[23]

Native peoples

American Indians and Alaskan Natives living near reservations have one of the highest suicide rates in the United States, according to the National Center for Injury Prevention and Control. Between 1979 and 1992 their suicide rate was one-and-a-half times that of the national rates and was especially high for young males between the ages of 10 and 34.[24]

Suicide among elderly Native Americans, however, is much lower than for the general population, which could be linked to the reverence shown their elders who gain stature as they age. However, Allen says it shouldn't be assumed that some of them are not depressed or suicidal just because they are revered.

In comparison to other races in the United States, Native Americans suffer higher infant mortality, cardiovascular disease, diabetes, alcoholism, and suicide, on and off the reservation.[25]

Indigenous Australians also show high rates of suicide among young people, particularly those between the ages of 15 and 19, but also, to a lesser degree, to those between the ages of 25 to 34.[26] Some suicidologists believe that the extremely high suicide rate among Native populations is due to the suppression of their religion and culture by prevailing governments. One example is seen in prisons where Native Americans have routinely been denied sweat lodge ceremonies, which is part of their religion, when other religious observances are acceptable. Canadian and U.S. prisons have only recently begun to allow the observances, although it isn't widespread.

Also, a study at the University of Denver attributed the high rates of suicide and other social pathologies, such as child abuse and alcoholism, among American Indians to the grief of massive losses of lives, land, and culture from European contact and colonization.[27]

Hyman has pointed out that Alaska is among the highest ranked states for suicide, and that American Indians and Alaskan Natives, who account for about 16 percent of the state's population, have suicide rates 70 percent higher than the established rate for the rest of the country.

People in certain parts of the United States

The Rocky Mountain states, plus Alaska and Nevada, have the highest suicide rates in the country. They include Nevada with 20.9 per hundred thousand, Montana with 19.9, Alaska at 19.8, New Mexico at 18.6, Wyoming at 18.3, and Colorado with 18.2. All are far above the national average of 11.6 per hundred thousand population.[28]

Federal government, state officials, and mental health experts are so alarmed at the high rates that in 1999, at a briefing in Washington D.C., Surgeon General David Satcher, M.D., announced the establishment of a National Research Center for Suicide Prevention in Las Vegas. Joined by the friends and families of people who had killed themselves, Satcher said that suicide has not received the attention it deserves, even though it is a leading cause of mortality in the country. He also spoke about overcoming the "unfortunate" attitudes of so many Americans toward mental illness.

He was joined at the press conference by Senator Harry Reid (D-Nev.), who spoke about his own father's suicide several years earlier, and the still prevalent stigma attached to suicide and mental illness. "I speak from experience when I say there is nothing more devastating than losing a loved one to suicide," said Reid. "After my father killed himself, my family had to bear the burden of that tragic experience in secret. At that time no one talked publicly about suicide, and there were no support groups to help us cope with our feelings." [29]

People with mental disorders

Conditions such as bipolar disorder are characterized by dramatic mood swings between mania and depression. The mood swings develop and subside spontaneously and may be cyclic, with sufferers remaining manic or depressive for months.

Many in the mental health profession believe the majority of potential suicide victims suffer from not only bipolar disorder, but also from undiagnosed schizophrenia or severe depression, and that medication and therapy are needed to get the person functioning rationally again. Brain scans show neurochemical differences in the brains of depressed people and those with other mental disorders. Their brains are simply wired differently.[30]

Many studies indicate that diagnosed schizophrenic patients have a high rate of suicide, up to 20 times the normal suicide rates in the areas studied. Dr. Cancro has urged his colleagues in the mental health profession to be more alert to the possibility of undiagnosed schizophrenia in young persons, as it manifests itself at a time when parents may believe the teen is simply having difficulty going through adolescence. "They think the teen will outgrow it."

"Parents have to learn to ignore the stigma of getting psychiatric help for their child," Cancro says. "Call the family physician and ask for the name of a psychiatrist knowledgeable about the disease. Parents are going to feel a lot worse if they don't get help. Some warning signs to look for include social withdrawal, falling off of grades, personality changes, and suspiciousness."

In *New Hope for People with Bipolar Disorder,* the authors write: "It is no surprise that the stigma of mental illness has been very strong in Western culture because our society places a high value on self-control, free will, and individual responsibility. Our society also expects us to exert self-control over our feelings and behavior. It is not difficult to see how these values, coupled with ignorance, have led to the public view of mental illness as a sign of character weakness."[31]

All strata of society

Although certain age groups, people living in particular areas of the world or the United States, or those undergoing personal trauma related to work or certain environments are targeted as higher risk groups, suicide still cuts a wide swath of tragedy and bereavement among all peoples and from all backgrounds.

Chapter 5

Confronting Depression

Depression is not isolated solely to modern man. The Greek physician Hypocrites wrote of the four humors—melancholic, phlegmatic, choleric, and sanguine—with Aristotle observing that melancholy seemed to attack the more gifted—an observation made today by some mental health experts.

Writing in *From Dawn to Decadence,* Jacques Burzun notes that Robert Burton, an Oxford don of the 17th century, emphasized the four humors and wrote that the melancholic seemed the most prevalent.[1]

Depression affects people in all cultures and doesn't discriminate against race, creed, or socioeconomic factors, although some studies show that the poverty stricken, especially in Third World countries, suffer most. One major reason, though, may be lack of access to mental health care. Yet, some of the latest findings show that New York City stockbrokers pulling down the biggest paychecks were also those suffering some of the highest levels of depression, burnout, and other afflictions.[2]

The Menninger Foundation in Topeka, Kansas, which is dedicated to advancing the cause of mental health, offers these little-known words of Abraham Lincoln on depression in *Menninger Perspective:* "I am now the most miserable man living. If what I feel were equally distributed to the whole human family, there would not be one cheerful face on earth. Whether I shall ever be better, I cannot tell; I awfully forebode I shall not. To remain as I am is impossible. I must die or be better, it appears to me."[3]

Whatever the label given depression, and whatever the underlying reasons for being depressed, it's been recognized as a major health problem that can sometimes lead to suicide or thoughts of suicide.

Some, but not all, of the contributing factors of depression can be stress, obesity (in women), genetic predispositions, abusive childhoods, anger, physical illness, traumatic events such as divorce, incarceration, low in dependency on others, aggression, mental and physical pain, and clinical mental disorders.

The World Health Organization's estimates for Global Burden of Disease says five of the 10 leading causes of disability worldwide, in both developed and developing countries, are the mental problems of major depression, schizophrenia, bipolar disorders, alcohol dependence, and obsessive compulsive disorders. As of 1998, major depression ranked fifth on the list, and is expected to jump to second place if the present trends continue.[4] In developed nations, including the United States, depression is the leading cause of disability.

Approximately 50 million Americans suffer some type of mental disorder, with 19 million of them afflicted with depression.[5]

Because the National Institute of Mental Health estimates that at least 15 percent of people who are suffering from untreated depression take their own lives, and approximately 30 percent of the population will suffer a severe depressive episode in their lifetimes (unlike mild forms of the blues that affect nearly everyone from time to time), the seriousness of depression can't be minimized. It's been estimated that depression costs U.S. companies

$24 billion annually, with the total cost of depression in the work-place at about $44 billion. Depression accounts for more than 50 percent of medical claims in companies, and it creates more days of disability than other chronic illnesses, such as diabetes or heart conditions.[6]

Even with those figures, neither federal or state legislatures have enacted legislation to force healthcare service providers and disability insurers to pay for therapy, although some states are now looking at such laws, or updates to existing insurance codes.

"We need to reinvigorate health clinics in schools. We also need more trained people in the schools. Mental health people should be in airports, post offices, and senior centers. We know where help should be made available. We know enough to know where this strikes," says Robert Dawidoff, professor of history at the Claremont Graduate University, Claremont, California.

Dawidoff, who wrote an op-ed piece in the *Los Angeles Times* on his own clinical depression, said the response to the piece was overwhelming. Still he asks, "But at what point does one have to end a life? I wonder sometimes. I'm not saying I'm coming out in favor of suicide, but I think not talking about the real issues involved keeps people from talking about suicide. You have to look it in the eye."

He says that even on campus, people don't talk openly if they are in therapy or taking medication because of fear about their jobs. But some co-workers and students talk to him, because he's been open about it. "People are dangerously isolated. If they could learn to talk more about this stuff, and if they needed help they would know where to go. We need to get mental disorder off the freak list and into the arts and crafts," he said. A portion of his op-ed piece reads:

Depression is still shameful. Everybody who admits to suffering from it—and it is an admission still—has heard the responses. I know just what you mean, today I had the most depressing experience... not realizing that those of us who suffer depression also have those bad days, rough times, misfortunes, and disaster, but that depression is something else, virtually a defining condition. Sometimes people tell us to just get over it ourselves, snap out of it, go to a movie—as if depression was lassitude and deliberate. Family and friends blithely question your taking medication or express confident doubts about your doctors and wonder if all that therapy is doing any good. They seldom have any useful alternatives in mind yet would be horrified and hurt if we replied, "OK, but will you deliver the eulogy when I kill myself?"

Dawidoff, who is gay, says that he's been discriminated against more for being "mentally ill" than for being gay. "I tend to be someone who is tough. I make people anxious. I think the major reason I'm discriminated against is because I'm a pain in the neck. When I do something, people say, 'He's crazy.' So I have experienced more discrimination about being clinically depressed."

What is depression?

Many of us suffer short periods of depression and some will experience only one episode in a lifetime. Others have them periodically, and in some cases depression is present most of the time. "Clinically depressed" means that a depressed person has a certain collection of symptoms that lasts more than two weeks.

The "blue" or "down" feeling experienced from time to time by nearly all people that is of short duration is not considered a clinical depression. The type of depression that can sometimes lead to suicide is clinical, affects about 19 percent of the population at some time, is not short term, and is treated by therapy, medication, or both.[7] Other conditions affiliated with suicide include bipolar disorders (manic depression) and schizophrenia.

Depression can begin as a seemingly short-term experience that lengthens in time, frequently triggered by an unpleasant event. Governments often send in mental health experts after natural disasters such as earthquakes and hurricanes, because those events can trigger severe anxiety and depression linked to posttraumatic stress disorder. One study in Florida, following Hurricane Andrew in 1997, found that those who experienced the greatest impact from the storm, such as losing their homes, suffered the greatest amount of depression.[8]

Many researchers believe that depression in the United States is an epidemic, and they note that a large percentage of the more than 30,000 suicides that occur annually in the United States involve people who are clinically depressed.

Some mental health professionals say that children as young as five suffer from depression, but their symptoms are difficult to recognize.

Most often, though, the first episode of depression is likely to strike women in their late 30s and men in their late 40s.

Depressive symptoms

Laurie S. says her depression was "like a wave. Then I would be fine, and then I would be back in the wave. Eventually, the wave didn't leave. I was paranoid. I felt like people didn't like me. I was living at my mom's, and one day I couldn't get up to go to work. I just cried and cried. Mom took me to hospital. They referred me to a doctor, and I tried three different medications. In the meantime, until they got the medications right, I would go to work and start crying. Mom would have to pick me up. It was really hard. You go talk to a counselor, and I still felt weird about that. I couldn't define why I was depressed. But, eventually, when we got the right medication, 'wow!' it was so much better. I was scared to go off the medication, but only took it for about a year."

She experienced another bout a few years later, but describes it as "milder." She took the same medication for a few months and has never experienced it again, but says she wouldn't hesitate to go to a doctor if she feels that wave coming on.

The experience has made her sensitive to others who are struggling with depression and not getting any help. "If I know someone who is depressed, I worry. If someone says, 'Oh, I just don't want to get up tomorrow,' I pay attention. Some people will think that's just an attention-getter, but of course it is. They need attention. They are saying, 'Help me, help me.'"

Counseling is good, she says. "But it also does depressed people good to talk to others who have been there. It helps to know that others have gotten through it.

"You can't just help yourself out of a severe depression. What you think is how you feel. You can't just say, 'I'm going to be happy today.' It's just not that easy. It's really a chemical thing."

Depressive symptoms can include feelings of fear or loneliness, irritability, lack of concentration, and sleeplessness, and they occur in 19 to 30 percent of people age 65 and older. Yet only one percent of those affected receive treatment, according to a Wake Forest University study. Also, women reported more depressive symptoms than men, even though elderly men are more at risk for depression. Married participants or those who lived with others had less depression. Smokers and those who had problems performing daily activities due to physical impairment had more depression, and so did participants who were inactive and overweight.[9]

Some studies show that menopausal women don't suffer any more depression than the norm. Others show them to be more prone to it. When it does lead to depression, researchers believe that more is at work than just a loss of estrogen.[10] Other studies show that estrogen replacement therapy (ERT) might help some menopausal women with depression, but chiefly only those who do not have major depression.[11] Another one indicates that for most women, menopause is not associated with depression, and if some depression is present, it dissipates by the end of menopause, regardless of the history of depression.[12] This is an area that needs a great deal more research.

Women as a whole, though, experience depression more often than men. It's believed that the cause, in part, is because women more often than men get caught in cycles of despair and passivity because of their lowered status in society, which leads them to ruminate about their feelings rather than switching to problem-solving skills.[13] This is true for young girls as well. Studies presented at the 1998 American Psychological Association Convention in San Francisco showed that adolescent girls worry about their looks, friends, personal problems, romantic relationships, families, and other concerns, while boys of the same age were more concerned about succeeding in sports and other activities.

Symptoms of depression include some, but not necessarily all of the following:

- Persistent sad, anxious, or "empty" mood.
- Feelings of hopelessness, pessimism.
- Feelings of guilt, worthlessness, helplessness.
- Loss of interest or pleasure in ordinary activities, including sex.
- Sleep disturbances (insomnia, early-morning waking, or oversleeping).
- Eating disturbances (either loss or gain of appetite and weight).
- Decreased energy, fatigue.
- Thoughts of death or suicide, suicide attempts.
- Restlessness, irritability, anger (especially teens).
- Staying mired in a crisis or loss that occurred several months previously.
- Difficulty concentrating, making decisions.
- Memory and attention deficits.
- Physical symptoms, such as headaches, digestive disorder, and chronic pain that do not respond to treatment.

If more than four of these symptoms are present, experts recommend seeking help through a physician, mental health specialist, health maintenance organization, community mental health center, state hospital, outpatient clinic, private clinic, or family service agency.

The sad fact is most people don't get proper treatment for any type of depression, either because they aren't aware of their symptoms, they've been misdiagnosed, they are engulfed in thoughts of the social stigma of "going to a shrink," or because many insurance programs don't pay for it.

Other reasons for resistance to getting help include denial that a problem exists, fear that a record of getting help might impinge on advancement at work, believing that no one can help them anyway, the fear of being institutionalized, lack of knowledge about what therapy consists of, cultural attitudes against seeking outside help, and previous unsatisfactory contacts with mental health professionals.

Depression is not normal in the elderly

The attitudes of some physicians is that depression in the elderly, and even some suicide, is a normal part of aging. This attitude deprives the aging population of what could be their finest years. Depression is a chemical process that can be treated, so that the elderly can live a quality life in the later years, rather than living at half mast.

Barry D. Lebowitz, chief of the Adult and Geriatric Treatment and Preventive Interventions Research Branch of the National Institute of Mental Health, says that depression is chronic and causes suffering and disability the same as diabetes, arthritis, and other illnesses common to older people. It is also contagious, becuase depression changes the mood around the entire household and affects those who live there. Unfortunately, because the generations of those past 55 were raised with an attitude that therapy was for sissies, they are often the least likely to get help. One 58-year-old man, whose girlfriend has urged him to get some help for his depression is, on the other hand, chided by his brother that it's nonsense. He just needs to "toughen up" and "quit feeling sorry for himself."

"If we have learned nothing else, we have learned that depression is a disease that is not a normal part of aging, and that it is not the expected normal response to all the stresses and strains of old age," says Lebowitz.

How a depressed brain reacts

Many in the mental health profession believe the majority of potential suicide victims are suffering from undiagnosed schizophrenia, bipolar disorder, or severe depression, and that in most cases, medication to get the brain chemicals functioning properly again is needed before traditional therapy can have any effects. Brain scans of depressed people show different highlights than those of normal subjects.

Certain brain chemicals—dopamine, serotonin, and nore-pinephrine—all called monoamines, send signals between brain cells, or neurons, and affect mood regulation, stress responses, pleasure, reward, and cognitive functions like concentration, attention, and decision making. People with bipolar disorder have an average of 30 percent more of monoamine-releasing cells even when they are not having symptoms. The brains of those with bipolar disorder are wired differently, setting them up from the get-go to bouts of mania and depression.[14]

Other studies include brain scans that are able to see emotions at work and pinpoint how they affect the brain.

Helen Mayberg, M.D., University of Toronto, says two parts of the brain work like the ends of a seesaw. When a person is experiencing strong emotions, blood flow increases in the brain's emotional center, with a corresponding decrease in the area that handles thinking.[15] But while the balance of the blood flow evens out quickly in healthy people, allowing them to snap out of their malaise, the imbalance persists in people suffering from depression. "Depression is a brain disease," she says.

"When people are intensely sad, the limbic areas light up and the cortical areas turn down (on brain scans). They work in concert. So that's why depressed people have trouble concentrating," she says. "They turn inward and don't pay attention to the outside world."

Part of this reaction is a survival technique for most animals when faced with grief. It allows time to readjust to the world. "If you're a little pup and you lose your mom, it's in the pup's best interest to not go exploring around. It's a time to take stock of the universe."

But the pup, like people, must eventually snap out of it in order to continue surviving. Some, however, can't snap out of it without help.

"We are an organism that is in tune to insure our own survival. Our bodies try to keep us alive at all cost, and the brain is no exception," Mayberg says. When the brain is lower in some needed chemicals, it tries to compensate to protect itself, and things can go awry.

Mayberg believes that the findings on how the depressed brain operates will lead to development of new therapeutic strategies where mood and cognition are affected. It also provides explanations for why psychotherapy might work for one person, while certain drugs are better for another, or why some need a combination of both, all of which can be monitored by brain scans.

Other studies show that two types of brain cells are abnormal in the prefrontal cortex just behind the forehead in people who have suffered clinical depression, most of whom eventually attempted suicide, according to studies at the University of Mississippi Medical Center.[16]

Long-term effects of chemical and hormonal imbalances in the brain, which can be responsible for depression, show that the size of the brain's hippocampus is smaller in women who have been clinically depressed when compared with women who never suffered a depressive episode. The hippocampus, part of the brain's limbic system, is affiliated with emotions and motivation and is involved in learning and memory.[17] Similar changes have previously been found in the hippocampus of patients suffering posttraumatic stress disorder.

However, researchers aren't certain if some people are simply born with a smaller hippocampus region that may predispose them to bouts of depression, or whether it is acquired as the result of years of depression.

Physical illness and depression

Other causes of depression can be physical illness, certain medications, and abnormal hormonal fluctuations. However, this can also be a "chicken or the egg" question, as it is not known whether physical problems cause depression, depression causes physical problems, or both.

Robert Carney, Ph.D., associate professor of psychology at Washington University School of Medicine in St. Louis, found that nearly one out of five coronary artery disease (CAD) patients had experienced documented incidences of clinical depression prior to their CAD diagnosis, and in the year following their diagnosis, these patients were twice as likely as non-depressed patients to have a major coronary event such as heart attack, surgery, or death.

Researchers at the university say that clinical depression may be as big a risk factor in CAD as cigarette smoking, elevated cholesterol, or high blood pressure. A depressed state increases mental stress, which may increase plaque formation and vessel blockages. Also, depression is thought to increase production of free radicals and fatty acids, which can damage the lining of blood vessels placing the person at higher risk for sudden death.

Some health experts think depression may affect the body to such an extent that it causes irregular heart rhythms or the progression of arteriosclerosis. Others suggest that depression might adversely affect motivation, and people stop doing the things that keep their bodies healthy, according to Carney. A 27-year study showed that the risk of heart attack or death from all causes increases in people who are chronically "blue."[18]

Even though the studies show connections between depression and health, earlier studies indicated that it was unknown whether treating depression in the elderly would reduce the rate of heart disease and death. More recent research, however, shows that therapy may reduce heart rate and increase short-term heart rate variability, cutting the risk for death in depressed heart patients.[19] Depression may also be associated with hyperglycemia in patients with Type 1 or Type 2 diabetes.[20]

"The first step is to identify the depression, and that tends not to be done in patients who have a medical illness. Studies suggest that two-thirds of people who have a psychiatric disorder on top of a medical disorder go unnoticed and untreated," says Carney. "There is clearly a mind-body problem in much of medicine, and there are major physiological changes that result when people are depressed," he adds.

Getting help

Dozens of different types of therapy exist to stop the cycle of depression. Some people may have the idea that therapy still consists of lying on a couch talking about their problems indefinitely. New types of therapy and medication, often in combination, can take care of the problem in 80 percent of people with severe depression far more quickly than is sometimes anticipated. Symptoms can often be relieved in weeks, and half of the people with major depression can be completely free of symptoms in four to eight months.

Ironically, several studies show that, on the whole, physicians take good care of their health, with low mortality from heart conditions, diabetes, and other chronic illnesses, but it surges when external causes are added because of their high rates of suicide.[21] Physicians, even when they recognize their own depression, are reluctant to go for help.[22]

Men, too, on a whole, are reluctant to seek help, says Frederic Rabinowitz, professor of psychology at the University of Redlands. "Therapy is often seen as a woman's place to work through problems. It involves verbalizing emotions and talking about problems, which are more common for women to do with same-gender friends, and it is thought to emanate from the relationship with their mothers, which is more interactive than a boy's with his father.

"On the other hand, boys and men tend to be less verbal and more uncomfortable in deep relationships. They tend to solve problems through 'doing' rather than 'talking.' Men are socialized to see expressing emotion (especially sadness and hurt) as being feminine and not masculine. Men are often brought up with a code that says if one shows these feelings or acts in a vulnerable way, then he is weak, a sissy, or a 'girl.' This shaming is pretty effective in shutting down men to opening up except to a rare few, typically a girlfriend, wife, or partner.

"Depression is experienced by many men as uncomfortable. Instead of wanting to talk about it, there is a tendency to try to do something to take away the feeling. Often this shows up as substance abuse (alcohol, drugs, cigarettes), obsessive activity of one kind or another (working, eating, gambling, TV watching), and often rumination (What could I have done? Why did I do that? I am so stupid. How can I get out of this?).

"To speak out loud about these activities or thoughts brings on more shame. Many men believe that if they don't talk about it, it will go away. The other route to deal with depression is to go to the general practitioner and say they need medication to 'pick me up' a bit. Rarely is there a direct acknowledgment, 'I feel depressed or down,' that might be more common for a woman to acknowledge," Rabinowitz says.

Some people respond to drug therapy, some to psychological treatment, and others to both. Exercise also helps to reduce depression and is used in some therapies along with drugs, and in some cases, successfully without drugs. No one treatment is perfect for everyone.

Those who are depressed, which can include survivors of suicide like Jean, get temporary help immediately. Others are able to cope without individual counseling, and maybe join a support group. Others wait many years and go for help when the loss of the loved one begins to interfere with their everyday life. Any person suffering from depression, including survivors of suicide, should consult his or her health provider, or seek initial help from religious affiliations or other sources of care and direction.

On the other hand, former suicidologist Adina Wrobleski said that not all survivors need therapeutic help. "Survivors of suicide need to recognize if their grief reaction is 'normal' or if it is in danger of becoming a serious depression. Many survivors say their greatest help came from taking part in survivors of suicide support groups."

Also, many physical conditions can cause depression, such as viral infections, cancer, head injuries, autoimmune diseases, and diseases of the thyroid, adrenal or pituitary gland. Also drugs, such as steroids, birth control pills, hypertension medications, and combinations of certain drugs can cause depression.

Behavioral therapies

Two types of therapies have emerged as the treatments of choice by a growing number of patients suffering from depression, and they are expressed in many different forms of individual therapy. Neither requires lengthy, traditional analytic approaches, and both have been scrutinized by the NIMH. These treatments may be used in conjunction with medication, depending on the response.

Both deal with the "here and now" and don't place emphasis on delving into the person's past. Neither is being recommended; rather, they provide a snapshot of some of the types of therapies being used to treat depression.

Interpersonal psychotherapy

One is "interpersonal psychotherapy," or IPT, which holds the view that depression is usually associated with the disruption of intimate relationships.

Interpersonal psychotherapy involves itself with four types of problems lending themselves to depression:

- Abnormally severe grief reaction over the death of a loved one.
- Interpersonal deficits involving socially isolated people.
- Interpersonal disputes caused by poor communication.
- Role transitions, created with life changes such as switching jobs or "empty nest syndrome."

Interpersonal psychotherapy studies indicate that women suffer more depression than men because they place a higher value on intimate relationships.

Gerald Klerman, M.D., former psychiatrist at Cornell University and a pioneer in the development of interpersonal psychotherapy, once said that "depressed people, including survivors of suicide, need help in dealing with unresolved grief. It's made more difficult for the survivor because of the stigma that's attached to suicide in our society and in most other societies."

The focus for the survivor is to learn to get on with life. "There is no blame for suicide. I'm not interested in blaming people. This isn't a moral judgment. We're interested in helping people cope better with their problems," said Klerman, in whose name the Gerald L. Klerman Research Awards are presented annually by the National Depressive and Manic-Depressive Association (NDMDA).

Large collaborative studies have been conducted by the NIMH comparing IPT, cognitive behavioral therapy, drug therapies, and placebos, demonstrating that IPT was effective in treating acute symptoms of depression during the first six to eight weeks, with improvements in psychosocial function continuing after 16 weeks. It was designed to be used without medication or in combination with anti-depressants.

Cognitive therapy

Cognitive therapy, another treatment of choice for depression, deals more with a person's own thought patterns, rather than relationships. Psychotherapist Gary Emery, pioneer in cognitive therapy and author of several books on the subject, says that basically, cognitive therapy emphasizes that depression stems from self-destructive, pessimistic patterns of thinking that usually develop over a lifetime. Patients are made aware of these patterns, and new ways of changing the distorted thinking that lies at the heart of the problem are instilled.

Cognitive therapy holds the view that the depressed person has a negative view of the self, the world, and the future.

"Researchers know what depression is. It is a clear-cut thing that can be measured," says Emery. "Depressed people tend to blame themselves rather than others, or the environment, for their troubles, and to personalize the problem—'It's my fault because...'— rather than treating it objectively."

Women tend to heap more blame on themselves and they underestimate their ability to control a situation, he believes.

"Men, on the other hand, tend to blame others for faults and overestimate their ability to handle situations. Mainly what cognitive therapy does is get you to stop thinking about your problems. Get the focus off yourself. Off your concerns."

Cognitive therapy can also be used for survivors of suicide. "At first survivors really aren't in a state of mind where they can make sense of the situation," says Emery. At this state, which may wax and wane for some time, there may be no need for therapy because grief and depression are normal reactions to loss. But Emery believes survivors need to refocus their thoughts once they're past the initial stages of grief. Emery disagrees with some professionals who say survivors need to ventilate their feelings. "I really think the main thing is not to continually think about the situation. Maybe initially it helps, but after that it's not good. It only stimulates the negative feelings," Emery says.

He adds that it's "unhealthy" for people to be grieving several years after the suicide and that if it's caused by guilt, they should remove it, along with other negative emotions.

"People sort of believe they should feel guilty. It's not necessary or useful. It doesn't help anybody. These [guilty] thoughts are really like behavior. If you don't reinforce them, they won't come back. If they keep coming back, it's because the person is attending to them.

"The other thing is, when thoughts come through, they are just thoughts. The reality is that the [suicide] is bigger than any of your thoughts," he says.

Eastern tradition therapies

Cognitive approaches are, in some way, similar to Morita Therapy, a Japanese therapy used by a few in the United States. Morita therapy emphasizes physical and mental action to overcome psychological problems. It is incorporated into an overall program called "Constructive Living" developed by David K. Reynolds, Ph.D., trained in anthropology. He says that one of the basic principals is to accept our feelings as they are, then go about changing our life circumstances if that needs doing. If we feel depressed, then we accept those feelings, but at the same time take steps to accomplish what we must. We co-exist with the unpleasant feelings of life. We really have no choice, he believes, because we can't "unfeel" our feelings.

Constructive Living is also composed of Naikan, a strategy that helps us look at how we're supported by the world all the time in practical ways. "For example," says Reynolds, "conversation is made possible by thousands of people. We don't know all their names, yet somebody at the telephone company is helping. Somebody taught us how to use the language we're using. Somebody went to the trouble to educate us for the skills we have. And two people gave me this body. So I don't have to look at life in some abstract, philosophical way."

Reynolds said that one of the general principals of the therapy is the notion that "The feelings of anguish, rage, and abandonment that survivors of suicide have are natural and don't need to be fixed. These feelings are generated because the survivors are ignoring the support of the world that we rely on for everything else.

"The strategy is to accept feelings as they come up, and there is no need to work on them, which is a little different than the Western tradition of trying to 'fix' all feeling.

"One can expect the feelings to fade as time passes. That is the natural condition, provided over time that things don't come up to restimulate them. We recommend that once the initial grieving is over, and they have talked about the experience and how awful it was, then we don't recommend they spend a lot of time restimulating the feelings by talking about them. One is to get on with one's life," Reynolds said.

Drug therapies

Dawidoff, who suffered severe clinical depression, says that what medications really seem to do is get you through a bad time. You can take a few steps back from the abyss.

"That's the abyss and I'm not going there. But I do remember when I took this medicine that it removed a certain kind of suicidal thought that I should kill myself. Most people wouldn't think I'm depressed, but for years I had that impulse and I don't have it anymore. What I have now (with medication) is just a plain depression."

Particular drug therapies are too numerous to mention, with more than 100 due out in the year 2001 for mental disorders, and more than two dozen of them just for depression. They are often prescribed in tandem with counseling, at least until the person is able to handle the situation without the assistance of medications.

Some people, however, need to maintain on medications throughout their lives, and it is difficult sometimes for a variety of reasons. Some, such as many of the homeless (who are often taking medications for schizophrenia or bipolar disorders), do not continue their medications when they are away from in-house care, or at least under close surveillance.

Others don't want the stigma of being a "pill popper" attached to them, or the stigma of having others know they are clinically depressed and need the medication to maintain a normal, functioning balance in life. And others, particularly those medicated for mental disorders, believe after a time of normalcy that they don't need the medication. A friend on a cruise told me of an incident that happened aboard ship. A young man on board, who seemed to make friends wherever he went and with whomever he met, was fast becoming the life of the party. By the second night on board, he was acting a bit drunk, and later in the evening ended up having to be restrained by staff for his wild talk and actions, culminating when he struck another passenger. He acknowledged the following morning that he had felt so good, he decided his medication for diagnosed manic depression was no longer necessary. He apologized profusely, and said it would not happen again. His shipmates understood, and everything returned to normal. He was still well liked by everyone.

One of the most promising new additions to the family of medications for clinical depression may be a surgical implant, the Vargus Nerve Stimulator, approved in 1977 for the treatment of epilepsy. It is about the size of a stopwatch and is implanted in the upper chest during outpatient surgery. Guide wires are tunneled up the neck and wrapped around the left vargus nerve, which connects to several parts of the brain involved in mood and emotion.

Whatever the method of administering antidepressants, and most are now taken orally, a Swedish study in 2000 showed that taking them reduced the rate of suicide in Norway, Denmark, and Finland up to 25 percent. The study was conducted in accordance with an increase in the administration of antidepressants. [23]

Exercise

Exercise is another mode of therapy, and in some studies has been shown to be as effective as some medications in treating depression and keeping it from returning. James A. Blumenthal, psychologist and lead researcher at Duke University Medical Center, said that antidepressants may be a more rapid treatment than exercise, but that after 16 weeks of exercise, it was equally effective in reducing depression, and that it may be more effective at keeping the symptoms from coming back.

Blumenthal said he considers it an alternative for certain people, and it might be tried as a first line of treatment, rather than starting a person on antidepressants right away. "But it's different than writing a prescription. The people in our studies had already been diagnosed with major depression," he said. "But they had a proclivity to volunteer for the exercise, so that may have had an effect on the outcome, because it provides a measure of control over their own bodies." Also, volunteers would be more likely to stick with an exercise program than sedentary non-volunteers who might be directed by a physician to get physical.

The exercise was also done in groups, which could, in itself, offer relief, because having a support group has been shown to reduce depression. For their next study, "we want to compare home-based exercise as compared to group-based," Blumenthal said.

People taking part in the study are 50 or older, because that age group reports some of the highest rates of depression. It involved more women than men, even though men make up the majority of depressed individuals in that age group, including higher suicide rates.

Some individuals, however, not linked with any studies, have already reported drops in their depression because of starting an exercise program. Blumenthal said James Taylor, noted musician, has attributed control of his depression (which he said had driven him to the point of suicidal thoughts) to exercise.

Chapter 6

Historical
Perspectives

Suicide has been the subject of debate throughout recorded history. Today's debate may be more enlightened, benevolent, scientifically based, and compassionate, especially for the survivors, but it still, in many countries, clings to outdated and harsh outcomes for suicide victims and the survivors.

The oldest recorded suicides are among the ancient Egyptians, who approved of suicide, because they believed they were passing from one life to the next.

Louis I. Dublin, in *Suicide,* says, "In classical literature as in the sacred writing of the Brahmins and Buddhists, there is considerable contradiction regarding the morality of suicide. Most authorities, however, seem agreed that suicide was not considered a sin in the Greek or Roman State; that it was mentioned with a certain degree of admiration in ancient legends and in Homer; that it was opposed by Pythagoras and other early philosophers; that the later schools of Greek and Roman philosophy took a more lenient attitude; and that the Cynics, the Cyrenaics, the Stoics, and the Epicureans rather actively encouraged it. All these groups tended to regard life as of little importance, although their emphases on its value were quite different."[1]

Also, in Greek and Roman times, when self-murder was frequently viewed as an acceptable way to stand up for one's principles, we are schooled in the suicides of Socrates, Cato, and Seneca.

Historically, the ancient Scynthians, and later some Native Americans, Eskimos, Aleuts, and Samoans, accepted self-sacrifice among the elderly and the sick, especially if the groups moved around a great deal, and when food was scarce. On the other hand, some groups in certain parts of the world reportedly have never had any suicides, such as the Yahgans of Tierra del Fuego in Argentina, the Andaman Islanders (cluster of islands midway between Calcutta and the equator), and some Aborigine tribes in Australia.

Religion and history

There appears to be no early cultural or religious sanctions attached to suicide in the Old Testament. Dublin says there are only four (other authorities say seven) instances of individual suicide in the Old Testament: Samson, Saul, Abimelech (wounded by a stone cast by a woman in the siege of the tower of Thebez), and Ahithopheol (whose counsel was rejected by Absalom). All of these men were given ritual burials.

William Graham Sumner, author of *Folkways,* points out there was a general weariness of life in the early Christian era that accounted for the readiness to commit suicide, causing indifference to martyrdom.

"Men fled from the world; pessimism took possession of the people; there was the longing for a better life, the struggle for redemption from this world and from the sins of the flesh and the longing to come before the face of the highest God, there to live forever. It followed naturally that the list of illustrious Greeks and Romans who committed suicide was a long one.[2]

"Though suicide continued on a large scale during the first and second centuries and Romans of wealth and rank embraced it with astonishing frequency, the attitude of the Christian Church from the time of St. Augustine (the fifth century) diametrically reversed this situation, and during the time when the Catholic Church held sway in Europe, suicide was practically unknown," said Sumner. In the New Testament, the suicide of Judas is mentioned without comment in Matthew 27:3, as a sign of his repentance, but much later the church claimed that Judas' suicide was a greater sin than was his betrayal of Christ.

Dublin writes that, "The early Christians apparently accepted the prevailing attitudes of their time on suicide, particularly when persecution made life unbearable for them. The Apostles did not denounce suicide; the New Testament touched on the question only indirectly, and for several centuries the leaders of the Church did not condemn the practice, which apparently was rather common."

St. Pelagia and St. Jerome approved of some suicides. St. Augustine was the first to denounce suicide as a crime. By the time of Thomas Aquinas (the 13th century), suicide was considered not only a sin, but a crime as well. Aquinas carried it further and said a suicide was worse than a murderer because a self-murderer kills both the body and the soul, but a murderer only kills the body. This attitude prevailed throughout the Middle Ages and persisted until about the 19th century in England, and in some cultures lasted into the 20th century.

During the Middle Ages, the corpse was often mutilated, and through the 19th and into the 20th century, suicides were denied Christian burial. The body was dragged through the streets or hung on the public gallows, left out in the open to be devoured by birds of prey.

Religious bodies today take a variety of positions on suicide, but most take a more understanding attitude than in the past, despite admonitions against it. Hinduism, Buddhism, and Jainism have traditionally held a different view on suicide than Christianity, and one that is constantly under review. Suicide can be and has been interpreted differently by various denominations, sects, and cultures. In cases of severe illness, Buddhism, Confucianism, and Shintoism accept suicide, but it's rare in Hinduism.

The survivors in history

Many European countries decriminalized suicide in the 18th and 19th centuries, although it remained a felony in England until 1961, and in Ireland until 1993. Suicide is still considered a criminal act in most of the Islamic community. But until it was decriminalized in Western societies, the surviving family members frequently had to move from the community and establish new lives—if that were at all possible. It is no wonder that even today, given its historical background, suicide is often "hidden in the closet," despite the enlightened, more compassionate, and understanding attitude toward suicide today, especially from the scientific community.

The old attitudes may have been intended to deter suicide, but there were still instances of mass suicides during the Crusades; sporadic mass outbreaks of suicide among Christians due to religious hysteria, persecution, and catastrophe; and great numbers of suicide during pestilence, such as the bubonic plague, sometimes called "Black Death," that killed more than 25 million people in 14th century Europe, and millions throughout Asia, India, Persia, and Egypt.

As other church bodies, such as the Anglican Church, became more prominent, some developed more humane attitudes toward suicide.

The French sociologist Emile Durkheim wrote in 1897 that suicide must be looked at in its social context rather than isolated individual motives. He called suicide a normal reaction to a society that isn't fulfilling the needs of all its members.

Changes in attitude

Since the turn of the century, it has been physicians, psychiatrists, psychologists, sociologists, and the newer branch of suicidology and its researchers who have promoted a more humane attitude about suicide, although all haven't been in agreement with one another on the causes, preventive measures, and treatments. Bereavement groups were not at the top of the list until it was recognized just how much survivors suffered, and how it affected society as a whole.

Today's professionals involved in the study of suicidal behavior believe that we need to take a new look at society's perception of suicide. Societies have a strong belief that all suicide should be prevented. People are unable to condone a death that they find unacceptable. So when it happens, we don't understand that maybe all suicides can't be prevented. Some believe that the only way to prevent suicide is to improve the quality of life, but experts point out that "quality of life" is a subjective thing. We see people who appear to be on top of the world, with seemingly happy families, they are well employed, and they kill themselves. Then others, who seemingly have nothing, and who might be living on the streets under the worst of conditions, put up a strong fight for life.

Beginnings of a new approach

Attempts to unlock the mystery of suicide began in earnest in the United Sates in the late 1950s and early 60s. Ironically, it began in part with the introduction of psychotropic medications designed to control psychotic symptoms.

"What was noticed at that time was an increase in the rate of suicide among those who were using the drugs. Within the Veterans Administration hospitals it became a matter of great concern," says psychologist and internationally noted suicide expert Norman L. Farberow, who was asked by the government to investigate the problem. The Veterans Administration established a research center headed by Farberow and Edwin S. Shneidman, another psychologist. This occurred at a time when the country's entire mental health community had begun to expand, taking into its grasp an endeavor to uncover some of the mysteries surrounding suicide.

Some European nations, primarily England and Austria, had already begun extensive research on suicide prevention. The research on both continents awakened the interest of the general public. "One of our earliest interests was to do something to dispel the many taboos that surround suicide. We were concerned with attacking particular taboos that prevented people from getting help. For a long time it was considered to be a cowardly, weak, unmanly, or crazy act," Farberow said.

These taboos caused those who were suicidal to keep their suicidal thoughts hidden and to suffer the consequences.

"We were concerned that they should feel open enough about it that they would be able to announce that they felt suicidal and ask for help, and also that the people they would announce it to would not try to deny it, and turn away from those who were crying out for help," Farberow said.

Prior to conducting research for the Veteran's Administration, Farberow and Shneidman, with a grant from the National Institute of Mental Health, had established the first suicide prevention center in Los Angeles, now affiliated with the DIDI Hirsch Community Mental Health Center at the Suicide Prevention Center of Los Angeles. It was geared not only to prevention, but to research, training, and education, and it served as a prototype for others that were later established throughout the country. Here, some of the first support groups for survivors of suicide were established. Today, there are nearly 400 suicide survivor support groups through the country (see Resources).

"Suicide will always be with us. Probably some suicides can't be prevented, and I don't like to say that. But we'd like to have it at a minimal level," said Farberow.

The role of societies in suicides

Farberow adds that the moods of society have a lot to do with the suicide rate. In the last half of the last century, the rate hovered between 12 and 14 per 100,000 population, with the lowest point being in 1956 when it dropped to about 9 percent.

"That was a period of great affluence. The whole economy was booming. We had just come out of the Korean War. There was a tremendous feeling of optimism," he says.

Still, in 1997, the rate in the United States was slightly more than 10 per 100,000, and in 1999 it was nearly 11 and one-half per 100,000.[3]

There are many social issues to be addressed concerning suicide. It isn't only affluence and "good times" that will lower suicide rates. Much depends on the self-worth of individuals and whether or not they are accepted by society.

Several Congressmen have introduced bills addressing suicide prevention, and the 1999 yearly health report from the Surgeon General's office included the mental health of the nation for the first time. It called for more research and understanding of depression and suicide.

Internationally, the World Health Organization has become involved in suicide prevention by launching the "Global Strategies for Mental Health" in 1999 to ease the burden of mental disorders and neurological illnesses that currently affect millions of people worldwide. The thrust of the program is to improve the population coverage and quality of psychiatric and neurological care throughout the world, particularly in developing countries.

In order to educate the governments and populations of countries, WHO, with the World Bank and Harvard University, USA, have developed a new measure. The Disability-Adjusted Life Years (DALY) measures the overall burden of a disease by showing how many years of potential life are lost due to premature death from mental illness, and the years of productive life lost due to physical disabilities produced by mental disorders.

For 1998, the WHO report estimated that 12 percent of deaths and lost productivity due to disease can be attributed to mental disorders, with an estimated 23 percent in high-income countries and approximately 11 percent in middle-and low-income nations. WHO is also poised to fight the "stigma, misconceptions, and discrimination associated with neuropsychiatric conditions, as well as promote human rights of the mentally ill."[4]

Changes in help for the survivors

Along with the recognition of mental disorders that can lead to suicide, the International Association for Prevention of Suicide (IAPS) is stepping up its work for survivors of suicide.

"There have been a lot of changes, not so much in the way survivors are being helped, but in getting help to the survivors. And that is important, because this part of the entire suicide picture had been one that was sorely neglected, and one which focused, appropriately so, on the people who were suicidal, and that is going on full blast," says Farberow.

As it now stands, the United States and Canada lead the world in bereavement programs, so organizations such as the IAPS are focusing on Europe, especially parts of Eastern Europe where the upheavals have brought about exceedingly high suicide rates. In 1997, Russia's suicide rate was close to 40 per 100,000.

In order to encourage the necessity and usefulness of suicide bereavement, the IAPS initiated the "Farberow Award" for individuals who have contributed to the formation of bereavement groups. It is given every two years to recipients such as Onja Grad, a woman from Slovinia, who knew she couldn't get help from the government and established bereavement groups through the auspices of family physicians, who are usually the first to see the traumatic effects on survivors. Slovinia's suicide rate between 1985 and 1996 averaged nearly 40 per 100,000.

In contrast, there are currently nearly 400 agencies providing suicide bereavement help in the United States and Canada. This list has been gathered into a directory by the American Foundation for Suicide Prevention, whose objective is to mobilize help for the bereaved (see Resources).

Taboos

The taboos surrounding suicide are being dispelled, especially in Western cultures and Australia. It's not as much as desired, but it's getting more notice in scientific communities.

"These studies [genetic and brain] help to eliminate the taboos. When parents know that something happened in their child's brain, it makes it a little easier to deal with," Farberow said.

"However, in countries such as Spain, Greece, and Portugal, where deep religious beliefs are hostile to the idea of suicide being anything but a sin, it is more difficult to spread the word that help exists," Farberow said.

Although several of the world's religions absolutely forbid suicide, it doesn't stop it. A study at the University of Rochester School of Medicine shows that the suicide rate among those over 50 in the United States may be lessened by attendance at religious services.[5]

Some countries with strong religious/governmental restrictions that deny suicide even occurs in their countries actually have some of the highest rates. It's believed by some that the more openly depression and suicide are discussed, the more it reduces the risk of suicide.

Ethics, euthanasia, and technology

It is not unusual for someone diagnosed with a life-threatening illness to consider suicide or, in the later stages of the illness when a great deal of pain is present, to desire euthanasia. But the issue is not so simple. Societies, including the United States, are fragmented on the ethics of euthanasia. Assisting a person to die by administration of drugs is illegal in most states, but the courts in the past 10 years have softened their stance, and now allow the refusal of treatment by extraordinary measures. Many states offer a "Durable Power of Attorney for Health Care Decisions" or a similar document, so that individuals can determine if they want extraordinary measures used to keep them alive. But more than just the law is needed in any discussion on the legalization of self-inflicted or assisted suicide.

Although Oregon legalized euthanasia in 1997, reports from 1998 and 1999 indicate that it isn't widely used in relation to the total number of persons in Oregon who died. Patients who request assistance with suicide appear to be motivated by several factors, including loss of autonomy and a determination to control the way they will die.[6] The Netherlands, where it seemed euthanasia had been legalized years ago, actually legalized it in 2001. However, no physicians there have been prosecuted since 1993 for practicing assisted suicide.

Some of the stipulations for its legality call for making certain that the patient is undergoing unbearable and irremediable pain from an incurable condition; the diagnosis must be certified by a commission; the doctor is required to "know the patient well"; a second opinion is called for; a doctor could not suggest it; and the patient would need to be of sound mind, or to have had an advance directive.

In the United States, most states keep rejecting legalized euthanasia, medical groups deplore it, and medical magazines and journals editorialize against it. An editorial in the *American Medical News* deplored the idea that laws would make it legal for physicians to assist in suicide. "When a physician is brought in, something else is being borrowed, not to be returned—the integrity of the medical profession."[7]

Robert Gable, professor of psychology at Claremont Graduate School, says, "If we can control the birth process, we can control the death process," although not necessarily by euthanasia, he believes. Gable has worked with hospice patients, and he believes that not only does society need to address the misconceptions about suicide in order to prevent more of them, but that the issues need to be given a full airing in order to enhance the lives of everyone involved. He emphasizes that suicide is only one of the ethical questions that society must come to grips with, and that other issues, including euthanasia, birth control, abortion, and drug use and abuse, are all entwined in unresolved mystery and conflict.

Some drugs are helpful, as in the case of treating depressed or disturbed people, "but we don't yet have a rational policy on how we are going to use psychoactive materials. We have a policy of 'Just say no to drugs,' which sends conflicting messages.

"Our ethics haven't kept up with our technology. We are a high-information society where anyone can know anything. This means we are going to gradually increase and demand to control the quality of our consciousness. Society has to take a look at these issues. Religious bodies tend to be stabilizing forces in a culture. So just as the Catholic Church is wrestling with what to do about birth control, we're wrestling with what to do about death control. There is a place in culture for a stabilizing church, but it is technology that is dragging that church, kicking and screaming, into the 21st century. I'm not blaming the church. Technology is just way ahead of our philosophies. We only invent philosophies after technology. So we are left with unanswered ethical questions about suicide, and it's companion, euthanasia.

"Yes, technically, euthanasia is illegal. As it is now, it's being done all over the country even though it isn't popularly accepted. People don't realize the extent to which it is being done. Almost everyone says that when they are dying they want the choice. Many hospice patients are older patients dying of cancer. They're given morphine, which is opium. The sick rooms in this country are the modern opium dens, only they are dismal. You wouldn't choose that setting if you had a choice. What the mind sees is what we are prepared to see. If we had the choice, we would choose a place of beauty, we would die in a place with flowers, music, and friends. Yet, we let people die in darkened places—isolated with no friends around because we are afraid to deal with death," Gable says.

He believes that the new studies linking suicide with mental disorders are the usual transformation of stigmatization. First it becomes medicalized, and that's what's happened to many of the major issues we deal with, such as homosexuality, abortion, suicide, and euthanasia. "Homosexuality first was evil, then a medical disorder, and now a semi-acceptable lifestyle," he says, adding that we need to give the medical profession its due, because it is leading the way to more understanding.

In another scenario, part of the attractiveness of euthanasia is that our government will not sanction the use of pain killers that will do the job when someone is in such pain that death seems not only the only answer, but implores us to make it a right. The majority of us have not suffered pain so unbearable that we cry out to die. What right do we have to deny others an end to a suffering that we have not, nor may ever have to endure? On the other hand, if physicians were allowed to administer an adequate amount and the right kind of pain medications without becoming suspicious in the eyes of laws made by people who aren't at the bedsides of screaming patients, then we might not need to even acknowledge that euthanasia might be needed.

I've heard it said over and over, and the more I age I must agree: "It isn't that I'm afraid to die. It's the way I might have to die that is so frightening."

This fear of death is just one part of the conflicting emotions society has toward suicide. It is clear that suicide is not a single issue problem. It is related to a plethora of conditions affecting the lives of our multicultural, diversified society. It calls out for new understandings in many areas of life, and death.

Chapter 7

Religious
Perspectives

Gilbert E. Brodie of King's College in Canada says, in a paper published in *Death Studies,* that suicide can seriously undermine the self-esteem of survivors. "The experience of guilt and shame so often found among the survivors of suicide is not unrelated to the same feelings found in the battered or abused child or wife. All have been assaulted by loved ones. Time and again we are told by survivors that the guilt goes beyond what we are likely to feel after any other kind of death. What they are experiencing is not just the normal loss but also the inescapable intimidation of rejection."[1]

The intimidation is compounded when the survivors feel rejected by the church. This is infrequent today, however. Most religious communities, while not condoning suicide, empathize with the deceased and offer love and compassion to the survivors.

Many survivors report that their religious or spiritual group is one of the greatest sources of comfort in dealing with the tragedy that has entered their lives. A good portion of the clergy of all faiths recognize that a suicidal person is not rational, and therefore, not accountable for his or her actions.

On the other hand, some religious leaders acknowledge that within the church, no serious discussion of suicide takes place, and that the clergy skirts the hard issues of just what the act implies for the person who commits suicide.

Jewish tradition

Jewish tradition, unlike most Christian groups, set guidelines for mourning, and Rabbi Marvin Goodman of Foster City, California, believes they help, especially in the case of suicide, because they offer assistance at a time when the survivors have lost any conception of what's expected of them.

The guidelines include an initial seven days of mourning where the family members don't leave the house. People come to them bringing food and condolences. This is a period of intense mourning. No one expects the family to do anything, and the family is comforted because nothing is expected of them. Mirrors in the house are covered so that the person is free to deal only with his or her inward feelings. For the next 30 days the grieving is not so intense, but the family is free to not do anything. At the end of about a year, a ceremony to dedicate the tombstone—an unveiling—takes place. This signifies the end to the intense mourning period. "It isn't that the person will ever get over the grief of the death—you never wholly get over that," said Goodman.

Jewish ritual gave him direction when a youth he had known and worked with committed suicide. Goodman was out of the country for four months and was unable to take part in the funeral. But he conducted the tombstone dedication and said, "It gave me the opportunity to express my words and feelings. I hadn't been there to cry with the family when it happened."

Goodman felt particularly grieved because the youth, who had obviously been having problems for some time, never confided in anyone. "I thought I knew this kid. I worked with him for several years, and I saw this strong, popular, seemingly articulate kid, and found out he had all these problems he never told anybody about. It just tore him up inside, and he didn't confide in anyone. A suicide can't be blamed for what they have done. The good in that person's life certainly outweighs the tragedy," said Goodman.

Some Jewish scholars believe there have always been acceptable reasons for suicide, some of which are illustrated in the Bible, such as the attack at Masada where Jews took their own lives rather than surrender to the enemy. During the Christian Crusades, crusaders on their way to the Holy Land would attack Jewish communities and try to force baptism. Whole communities committed suicide rather than be baptized. "And during the Holocaust, we definitely know there were more suicides, especially those engaged in the resistance and couriers in the ghetto. They committed suicide rather than be caught and tortured," said Rabbi Ben Zion Bergman, professor Emeritus at the University of Judaism in Los Angeles.

Zdzislaw Ryn, M.D., of Poland, who researched war records, says that thousands of Jewish people killed themselves when conditions were at their worst between 1940 and 1942. [2]

In the past, Jewish culture has had one of the lowest suicide rates, but it nearly equals that of Christian culture today. Because of the growing problem of suicide, national Jewish task forces have been instituted to deal with the problem. "In general we are catching up with the general community in lots of ways. We used to also have a very low divorce rate. The changes are the price of our integration into general society. As we become acculturated to the specific demands and influences of the general culture, our traditions become less potent," says Rabbi Bergman.

Bergman says that the breakdown of the family contributes to the increase in suicide, "because the force of the tradition has been weakened."

Like the Christian tradition, Judaism has, through the ages, softened its harsh stand against suicide. "Every sin is forgivable in Judaism," says Bergman, but traditionally a suicide was treated as absolutely the worst of malefactors. The suicide victim wasn't buried within the burial ground and the early commentators forbade the eulogizing of the suicide. The family wasn't to observe the rites of mourning. By the 18th century, there was still no eulogy allowed, but for the family's sake they were allowed to observe the rite of the seven days of mourning.

In a later attempt to ameliorate the harshness of the laws, Jewish authorities said that while it was true that the person had done something to take his own life, it was unknown whether or not he repented in the instant before he took his life and it was also possible that he wasn't in his right mind—distraught with pain and not really responsible, according to Bergman.

"For the parents, it's easy for them to feel guilt, and I try to point out that there are many influences and forces at work today that are beyond parental influences. The thrust of today's Judaism is to give comfort to the family," he adds.

Christian tradition

H. Newton Malony, professor of psychology and theology formerly associated with Fuller Theological Seminary in Pasadena, California, agrees that the main responsibility of the church is to give comfort to the bereaved.

Those who have been raised with the ideology that suicide is a "deadly sin" should "put their reliance on a merciful God," says Malony. "God is simply more in the forgiving business than the judging business. Suicide is born out of great travail. Some have said it is an aggressive, hostile act, but I think it is a troubled soul who wants to get out from under the stress they're under. God is merciful there, although He doesn't take the sadness or mystery away, or the perplexity or confusion as to why someone would commit suicide. The Christian faith functions as a comfort, and it is no different in the ways we are confronted with other tragedies of life—the other perplexities and enigmas of life that don't make a lot of sense. You simply rest back on the sovereignty and mercy of God."

Malony believes that the most important question facing survivors isn't their perplexity as to why the person committed suicide, but the overall confusion and ambivalence survivors feel.

"The person simply has to let go, and that's tough," acknowledges Malony.

"What is going to happen to them? They're kept in turmoil because there are no real answers. I've heard survivors say they've felt the presence or the spirit of the suicide victim hovering around, and if it is a hostile presence, it is a frightening thing."

As well as counseling survivors, Malony had firsthand experience in dealing with suicide. First, when he was in seminary school more than 40 years ago, a close friend jumped out of a church tower.

"It led me to contemplate my own suicide, and I think that's part of the ripple effect—why sometimes you have one suicide following another. It led me to believe that if he doubted his faith, maybe I wasn't so sure of mine either. I was going through my own intellectual crisis at the time—'Do I believe in God?'—and I think that's pretty typical. You start asking yourself, 'Does life have meaning?'"

His friend's suicide shook up that belief because "part of your sense that life has meaning is that those about you also affirm its meaning. If that is shaken by someone close to you saying, 'Life doesn't have meaning, and I'm going to take myself out of it,' your buttress is shaken. That is the ripple effect. There is this implicitly unconscious dependence on this person confirming your existence. That's why there is so much anger associated with suicide, and I believe the anger is healthy. My understanding is that where that can occur early, as well as the sadness, the grieving is lessened. Anger is energy turned outward as opposed to depression, which is anger turned inward. So showing anger is much more healthy than turning inward and blaming the self. We could easily blame ourselves—'I could have done such and such'—but the thing is, the person is going to do it if he or she is going to do it. A person will find a way."

Later in life, Malony experienced the loss of another friend to suicide. Malony had officiated at the man's wedding several years previous to the suicide and when he had renewed his wedding vows, an event that took place only three days before the suicide.

"All things seemed to be going uphill for him," said Malony. "You do have to say that the Christian faith functions in several ways. One is comfort. Another is challenge, and another is the call to right living. But in this case, the Christian faith functions as comfort and it is no different in the ways we are comforted during other tragedies of life."

When Monette L.'s mother committed suicide and preparations were being made for her funeral, Monette candidly asked the officiating minister if he had any problems with the thought of conducting the services for her mother. She said that if he did have reservations, they would get someone else.

"I was ready to fight," she recalls, "But it wasn't necessary."

Speaking forthrightly about this saved the entire family much grief. They were assured that the services for their mother would be carried out in a dignified and loving manner.

Father Peter Covas, pastor of St. Peter and St. Paul Catholic Community in Alta Loma, California, said the change occurred about 35 years ago. Prior to that, it was considered a "public scandal," and burial within the church was forbidden.

"The thinking now is that when the person reaches the stage where they are really contemplating suicide, they're not in control of their real faculties. So before God there is no offense," he said.

"That is one place where the church has more or less changed its attitude," said Sister Jane Frances Power, former director of Health and Hospital Department for the Archdiocese of Los Angeles and Founding President of the Board of Directors of the Serra Project, a supportive outreach program established by the Archdiocese in 1987 that assists and houses people living with HIV/AIDS. Power is now retired but active as an advisor to the project.

"It used to think it [suicide] was a deliberate thing, and was therefore sinful. But it has been many years since that attitude was held by the church. The proof of that is that they say a memorial mass for the individual. When I was young they didn't say that mass. They used to think the person was totally in their right mind when they did it, but we know today that they do it under different circumstances and aren't competent. As far as condemning them and saying they are going to hell, we don't do that. The individual state of mind is what determines that and that is between the person and God.

"I would counsel anyone the same as with any other bereavement. Of course, if they feel that the loved one did something wrong, that is a terrible burden to bear. I would emphasize that the person was under stress and strain and that his motives are left to God," adds Sister Jane Frances.

Some Protestant groups believe suicide is a sin, but not an unforgivable one, and still other Protestant bodies believe that suicide has nothing to do with the person's relationship with God. Some, like former Presbyterian minister Covell Hart, believe that many people who commit suicide really have no desire to die. They are reaching out and struggling.

He knows firsthand of what he speaks, because Covell attempted suicide several years ago when his first wife asked for a divorce. He went out to the garage, closed the door, turned on the car's motor, and waited to die. "It was about 2:00 a.m. and this widow lady who lived down the street was driving home and her car died. She got out to see if she could get help at our house because the lights were on. She heard the engine running, looked through the garage door, saw me slumped over the wheel, and went and got someone to help break down the door."

Covell was unconscious for a couple of days in the hospital. An unusual twist to his story is that right after he got out of the hospital, he received a phone call from a friend in New York that he hadn't heard from in 20 years. The friend said she woke up in the middle of the night and was obsessed with thoughts of him. She woke up her husband and he joined her in prayer for Covell without even knowing what had happened.

Because of his experiences, Covell believed it made him more understanding when he dealt with any type of trauma confronting a family, especially because at the time of his suicide attempt and subsequent divorce, the church body he was affiliated with offered little support and comfort. He changed his affiliation, and eventually served other ministers of various denominations who were faced with adversity in their own lives, and who needed support.

His wife, Phyllis Hart, also an ordained minister and a psychologist, recalls that she learned about suicide the hard way, and from those experiences developed a more enlightened attitude about it. One event involved a young couple who were her friends. "The husband was a super guy and he died suddenly of a freak illness. Several months later, the wife was extremely depressed and seeing a psychiatrist. Nevertheless, she took her youngest child into the garage and told him they were going to go see his daddy. She spared her two older children. The younger child died in her arms of carbon monoxide poisoning.

"We should have paid more attention to her depression. We even said we 'should have done this… should have done that.' It was a tremendous devastation."

Another event that caused Phyllis to take a second look at suicide occurred early in her career, when she was working at a psychiatric facility. One of the patients, whose husband of many years suddenly walked out of their marriage, was continually asking about suicide. "She seemed too crazy to commit suicide and we disregarded her comments such as, 'If I put a rope around my neck will I die?' Well, the woman did commit suicide. We learned a lot of lessons from her. We know now to pay attention. Those who are left have to deal with the guilt."

Although the mental health community today is pretty well agreed that the leading cause of suicide is mental disorders, some church bodies still cling to age-old beliefs about its cause, as do some individuals. Even for those who understand the breakdown of the mind leading to suicide suffer the same devastating effects, such as sadness, grief, and anger. But it is anger that is stifled, and which can create effects that may drag out the bereavement period. Recognizing that anger is normal and to get it out is the best route, Phyllis said.

The entire area of grief over a suicide death is muddied. "There is a kind of popular view that grief is only supposed to take a certain time, but this is not realistic. It is a recurring emotion. Grief is not a constant emotion, and the less you have dealt with it intensely, it will stay relatively untouched and pop out every once in a while," Phyllis said.

In the book, *After Suicide,* John H. Hewett, a Baptist pastor, said that the survivors need to rid themselves of the superstition that suicide victims go to hell. "This often results from a rigid logic that teaches that forgiveness occurs only after repentance. I believe the wealth of the Biblical evidence shows that God's grace and mercy are unmerited, given freely. We don't earn his love, we receive it."[3]

Buddhist tradition

A friend, whose husband deserted her when she was 45, went into a deep depression for several years. Many of us feared she might try to take her own life. One time, she acknowledged that, "I was seriously considering it a few months ago, but an acquaintance of mine told me that if I committed suicide, I'd have to come back in the next life and live this one all over until I came to terms with it. The idea of having to live this life over again is worse than going on with it now."

Her belief is based on misconceptions deriving from the Buddhist faith, which believes in reincarnation and karma. Buddhism, which had its origins in Central and Eastern Asia in the sixth century B.C., teaches that right thinking and self-denial enables the soul to reach Nirvana, a divine state of release from misdirected desire.

Like most faith groups, including Christianity and Judaism, Buddhist scholars disagree about the extent of suicide being acceptable. A recent entry in the *Encyclopedia of Religion* states,

"Buddhism in its various forms affirms that, while suicide as self-sacrifice may be appropriate for the person who is an arhat, one who has attained enlightenment, it is still very much the exception to the rule."[4]

One of Buddha's disciples, Godhika, is said to have achieved advanced levels of enlightenment to the point that when he committed suicide, Buddha blessed the action, while at the same time cautioning his other disciples against suicide.

"Each individual has the responsibility to maintain his or her own life, and one is not given the authority to kill others or themselves. But if they do commit suicide, if they can't face the problems of life, it is their responsibility and not that of the survivors," said the Venerable Dr. Havanpola Ratanasara, former president of the Buddhist Sangha Council of Southern California.

"With the Buddhist teaching, life is a continual process. In the course of one's life, certain things in the previous life follow the person, due to their karmic results." But he said it doesn't necessarily mean the person will come back in another life to finish the one they didn't complete. "We don't know what karmic influences they will have in their next life. We think life, as a whole, is a continuous flux. Life itself doesn't end with the death, so as long as there is a desire to the attachment to life, then life will continue.

"If the person has done something really morally good, he is sure to be born again in a good state. That is one thing. The other thing is, Buddhists are not equipped to feel bad about death. We are experiencing it at all times. Life has three characteristics. One, arising; two, existing; and three, dying—one after the other. We don't see all this through our eyes, that everything is changing at all times, so when things do change we become sad. But one shouldn't be sad. There is not reason to grieve yourself.

"When a person comes into the world, they are alone. They don't give any notice that they will be here on such and such day, and what they are to be named. It is purely individualistic, and the kind of relationships one deals with in life aren't the permanent things. Relationships are built after birth. Once the person dies, these relationships are over. A person shouldn't get strong attachments to life or to anything. Follow the middle path and don't get unduly attached to anything. Learn to understand the nature of change.

"The suicide is not a free man, so they are to be pitied," Ratanasara said. "Sure, we feel sorry for the person, but we understand the realities of it. It is human nature to feel sorry, but we don't continue to do it."

Offerings, or the practice of dana, whereby food is brought to the temple where the monks live, and a ceremony that is performed, are the two rituals practiced in the name of the departed. But the practitioners know the deceased will be back in another life, so they don't worry about him, according to Ratanasara.

Many people in Western culture may find difficulty accepting Ratanasara's views, because they may seem harsh to some. Few survivors, however, would argue that they want to get on with life. That's why it's important to listen to the survivors, because they are the ones who hold the key to greater understanding. It is they who have forced society's religions to come to grips with suicide, and to bring it out into the open for a long overdue airing.

Islamic tradition

A study in Pakistan reported in the journal *Crisis* challenges the widely held belief that suicide is a rare phenomena in an Islamic country. Like elsewhere in the world, the numbers of male suicides surpasses that of women. Traditionally, Islamic countries do not report suicide, according to the World Health Organization, which carries few statistics on most countries affiliated with Islam.[5]

Like many of the world's religions, however, where suicide is considered an affront to God, the benevolence of God is invoked. Shahid Athar, M.D., Clinical Associate Professor of Medicine at Indiana University School of Medicine, a Muslim and a Pakistani, says that because the Koran and Prophet Mohammad clearly say that suicide is forbidden, it does help in also keeping the rates lower than in many other countries.

On the other hand, suicide does occur, but those who are educated and knowledgeable know that people are not mentally competent when they commit suicide and are, therefore, not responsible for the action, Athar says.

"The Koran clearly says don't take your own life. Sanctity of life is very important. But another belief that we have is that anyone who takes his own life, his fate will not be decided right away. His soul won't be taken to heaven or hell until God decides what to do with him. Real bad criminals will go to hell right away, and a good person will go to heaven right away, but a person who commits suicide will need to wait."

Athar said the most common groups who commit suicide in his country of birth are women in abusive marriages, youth who feel too restricted by their parents, two lovers from different classes or tribes who are forbidden to marry, and a man who struggles but fails to support his wife and children. He says that in America, when wives or youth are presented with similar problems, they can move away, but that's not possible in many Muslim countries.

If a Muslim child commits suicide, "the parents will be depressed and grieve. It's very sad, but they won't suffer endlessly with guilt. They won't feel ashamed. We are told that after a person dies not to speak badly of them. So we don't really talk much about it," Athar said.

One of the major problems in Third World countries, he says, is that the uneducated will not seek help for mental problems. Even in America it's a taboo subject, he says. People are afraid to go for help, because it will become part of their medical record and maybe prevent them from obtaining a job or a promotion.

"By the time people have been driven to an extent that suicide becomes an option, they will say that nothing is wrong. And if people are at that point of being distraught and hopeless, they won't turn to their religion. Usually people who are that depressed have been that way for a year or more," he says.

Adding to the problem is ignorance of what psychiatric treatment can do to restore a person to rational thinking. "You can control some conditions with prayer, but a person needs medication for severe depression," Athar says. "People don't think the brain can get sick just like the heart and lungs, but it does. And the cure for depression may not be permanent. Some illnesses, just like arthritis, can't be cured permanently. So it's a complex problem."

It's not only difficult to get people to seek treatment for depression that can lead to suicide, but it's difficult to deal with it through a person's religion. "A person who takes the life of someone else, in our opinion has committed Shirk, and that means associating with the powers of God. They are trying to be like God. Yet, the person who commits suicide can't be blamed. That is the decision of God," Athar said, adding that as physicians, "we wish we could have gotten him earlier. Friends and the family have an obligation to recognize the symptoms early. Most people deny the depression. They should recognize it early and help the person seek treatment with more than just prayer."

Hindu tradition

The modern Hindu faith appears to place a taboo against suicide, although there is a long history of suicide associated with bereaved widows killing themselves in the funeral pyre, sometimes aided by the families (Sati). Also, "altruistic" suicide, such as starving oneself for a cause as Gandhi did, or in ancient lore, killing oneself in battle, or committing suicide rather than being taken captive, were once acceptable.

Hinduism claims to not be a religion, but a type of wisdom that some scholars liken to humanism. Hindus consider themselves to be responsible for salvation, which involves liberation. It is achieved by good acts and asceticism.

Gandhi is one of the tradition's most notable adherents. He said, "Identification with everything that lives is impossible without self-purification; without self-purification the observance of the law of Ahimsa must remain an empty dream; God can never be realized by one who is not pure of heart. Self-purification therefore must mean purification in all the walks of life."

Also, he said, "Reason follows the heart, it does not guide it. A pure heart is thus the most essential requisite for mental and physical health."

Nalini Juthani, M.D., a Hindu, and director of psychiatric education at Bronx Lebanon Hospital in New York said, "My being on a spiritual path means I can relate to people of any faith in a non-judgmental manner. I try to identify with their religious beliefs, and integrate it into treatment."

Juthani said she deals with people of all faiths, and from the onset of their treatment, attempts to find out if they are spiritual or religious. One of her patients had attempted suicide seven times. Through treatment, he became aware that maybe a higher power had a mission in life for him, because his attempts had been unsuccessful. "That idea became a very powerful thing in treatment. Today he has become very involved in his church," Juthani said.

She became interested in the effects of religion on a person's health many years ago, and developed an evaluation of where a patient's faith fits into recovery. She has received awards from the National Institute of Health Research, a group that promotes religion into healthcare, for her work.

Patients were asked 1) if they believed in a higher power, 2) if they practiced their religion by going to a worship service, 3) if they prayed, 4) if their religion or faith had helped them (or hurt them), and 5) how their religion and faith had helped them in times of difficulty.

Juthani said she has discovered that those who believe in a tyrannical type of God don't do as well in treatment and afterward as those who experience a more loving God.

Her observations and research are in keeping with other studies that show religions that have historically evolved into the concept of a more loving and less tyrannical God promote the psychological health of people more readily than those that adhere to a tyrannical God.

The major religions throughout the world have continuously evolved throughout history in keeping with the times. Most of them today, while not condoning suicide, have far greater understanding of the medical and psychological causes of suicide, and readily offer comfort and understanding to the bereaved, and compassion for the suicide victim.

Chapter 8

Preventing
Suicide

The following letter, a cry for help, was sent to me after a series of articles I wrote on suicide appeared in a Los Angeles area newspaper. The 15-year-old girl who wrote it indicated she had contacted a crisis center in her area, which can be a first line of defense in preventing suicide.

She wrote:

There are many things to prevent suicide. If people did not have troubles they would not need suicide. I have thought of it many times because of not having someone to talk to. So all I did was called the Suicide Prevention and it helped me a lot.

I am 15 years old. My problems all started with my parents. Me and my parents get along but sometimes they tell me not to do something and I do it anyway. I understand why they get mad at me then. Sometimes they get mad at me because they are mad at someone else.

I have an older brother and an older sister and a younger sister, so I am just pushed away.

Mental health experts say that most suicidal people give warning signals. These signs, however, often don't register on our conscious minds until after the fact—then it's too late. Even when hints are given, most people are hesitant to broach the subject or to ask the direct question, "Are you thinking of committing suicide?" Those words aren't in our lexicon, and they are difficult to utter.

Dealing with the pain

Elaine G. of Las Vegas was 18 when she attempted suicide. At 25, she spoke out about it. She had many of the danger signs and was in counseling at the time. In retrospect she said:

"I didn't really want to die. I just wanted to end the pain. I was in counseling for quite a while before the suicide attempt. I was really messed up. I guess I was looking for somebody to scream out to help me, but it wasn't working. I didn't think anybody understood and it wasn't getting through. I was no longer just thinking about it. It was something I wanted to do. I don't know where the idea for the suicide came from. It was just there. It just came. It was as strong as the urge to live must be. It seemed just another instinct. I thought about it for so long and finally, I no longer thought about it. I said, 'This is what I'm going to do. I'm not happy. I don't want to live. You know you're not going to get run over and die, so you just have to go out and do it yourself.'"

Her stay in the hospital after the attempt changed her thinking. "It shook me. I realized a lot when I was in there. I still had the same feelings. They didn't go away. But I didn't like being locked up in that place. I missed little things—to come and go and to sit outside and talk to friends. I asked myself, 'Do I really want to lose all this?'"

Her counselor was "shook up" about the attempt and told Elaine that she (the counselor) had lost her objectivity. "She told me she was too close to the situation."

The two are still friends, and Elaine frequents the same counseling center, but sees a different therapist. Elaine believes this is why parents and close friends can only listen and guide you to professional help when a person begins talking about suicide.

"You have to talk to someone who can be objective and not give opinions of how wrong it would be of you to commit suicide. Statements such as, 'But you have so much to live for,' or 'Why would someone like you want to commit suicide?' have no meaning to the person who is engulfed in suicidal thought."

She was 20 when she went back into counseling. "For a while I just sort of existed—went with the flow. My life didn't get better, and I had to see if I could make it better. Things started coming around. My perception changed. I just started enjoying life again. I was still doing drugs, but I was older, out of school, and I wasn't suffering from the pressure of school." Although Elaine was still taking drugs, she was able to look back on the suicide attempt and say, "How could I have done that? Life is a growing process and every day I began to appreciate life a little more. It took time to work through and let things change."

Elaine was finally able to give up drugs, although she said it's a continuing battle, and she occasionally slips back into counseling for needed support.

"Drugs didn't make me attempt suicide. The life and the past memories that I hadn't dealt with helped cause the suicide attempt."

Elaine's statement is supported by health professionals who say that drugs and alcohol don't cause suicide. They simply lower the inhibitions about going ahead with plans to end a life. Using drugs and alcohol is just another way of trying to deal with the pain and hurt of what's going on in a person's life.

"Most people who do drugs do it for a reason. They're trying to cover up something or get a feeling they can't get anywhere else. They don't do drugs just for the heck of it, and they don't do drugs just because the other kids are doing it. Until I got counseling I didn't realize there were more serious reasons. And some of those same reasons led to the suicide attempt. It's not one thing. It's a hundred things that build on you and make you do it. You've got to just hang in there and get help. If it takes going to 20 people before you find somebody that makes you comfortable—a qualified professional—then it's worth it," she said.

Elaine believes it's okay to reach out to parents and friends, but that's only a beginning. By the time a person is contemplating suicide, he or she needs professional help. Parents and friends can listen, and then encourage the person to get in touch with a professional.

"If I hear someone say, 'I wish I was dead,' I don't take that as a light remark. And I don't beat around the bush. I just ask them if they're contemplating suicide. If the person thinks someone cares about their problem, it helps. Just listen to them. Tell them you love them and what to do to get help."

She acknowledges that some people think they don't have the money to pay for counseling. "But the fact is," she says, "There is help for everyone." Most states have programs that assist in counseling fees, and some states are working to see that insurance companies offer some type of payment to cover therapy.

Friendship

T. Wilson, whose first suicide attempt was at 16, says about friendship, "I know from experience and talking with a couple of other people who have thought about, or attempted suicide, that having someone who cares enough to listen can help. If they would just say they were willing to listen and sat in closer proximity and touched your arm, you would know they were paying attention— 'I'm here. Feel me.'"

She says comments such as, "Aw, come on." "Get off it." "Have you eaten today?" and other comments that make light of depression or suicidal talk are extremely irritating to a suicidal person.

"Better to say something like, 'How strongly do you feel like doing it?' or 'Should we get some help?' or 'Do you just want to talk?'" she said.

Wilson attempted suicide twice when she was 16, and says she would have tried a third time, probably successfully, if she could have found the bullets to her grandfather's gun that he kept in the house.

By the time Wilson was 21 and attending college, she still occasionally had thoughts of suicide, but said she had enough support systems to help her through the episodes.

No one knew of her first attempt when she took "bottles of pills" and went to bed expecting to die. The pills made her sick, and she threw them up later in the night.

The second attempt, also as a teen, involved slashing her wrists. A friend took her to a doctor who simply treated the wounds and dismissed her without asking how she got the cuts. She was living alone at the time, and it wasn't until she was 18 and living with her grandparents that she sought help from a professor who was teaching a psychology class that she attended. The professor directed her to a counselor at the school and she began therapy.

"It's been a rough road going through counseling. In our family, we have a rule that you don't talk about your emotions. None of them know to this day what I went through. But I've developed my own support group, and I'm involved in a Bible study class where I have some friends. I can say to them, 'Hey, I really feel down. Let's talk or do anything.'

"Some of my friends know about my suicide attempts, but they don't know the circumstances and haven't asked. I've never really said much because it's been so hard. I hate to admit, even now, that I have these thoughts. I'm on medication for depression, and I used to have hang-ups about taking the medication."

But the psychiatrist she was seeing at the time of the interview was helping her through that. "He doesn't hold any judgment and that's a big help. A supportive family would be a big help, but I've come to terms with the fact that I will never have that."

Keeping a journal, which Wilson did since the age of 13, helped. She was an abused child. "If you can't talk about it, at least you can write about it, and it's been a big help. Once I get it out on paper, I start looking at other ways in life that I can handle it."

Here is one of the poems, titled "One Night," that she wrote at age 16 and entered in her journal:

I sat on the bed
waiting for the right moment
Soon.
Very soon.
I had made sure everything would be right
the razor
silver and sharp
gleams against the candlelight
Soon.
Very soon.
I won't make a sound
the razor's edge
gliding on the skin of my wrist
at last I feel the warmth
that I've always wanted to feel
the dark red blood runs down my arm
and now the next wrist.
The beauty of the blood
seen by the candlelight
is kind of lonely with no one to see my ecstasy
oh, well, no big loss.
Soon.
Very soon.
my misery will end
no more
my misery will end

"The poem seems gruesome now. I certainly see that now, but I also see that I needed warmth. A simple hug would have been great, especially at the time I wrote it," she said.

"I keep wondering why I never put a period on the last line of the poem. I don't know if that was a statement in itself, or what."

Stages of suicide

Not all suicide is impulsive. Some research suggests that suicides evolve over at least a 90-day period, while planning proceeds in an orderly process. Three distinct stages have even been identified. The longest phase, during a period of agitation and restlessness, is considered the "resolution phase." People struggle with the moral and ethical issues involved. They even might wonder what effect it will leave on loved ones.

A second, shorter phase is less agitated, while they wrestle with how they will do it. The person thinks about who might discover them.

The third stage is the one noted by many survivors. The person seemed calm, and the survivors were relieved if they had been concerned, or were happy to see the person in such a good mood. That's when we hear, "I had no idea." "He was in the best mood I'd seen him in for months." Also during this third stage, the person may get things in order and give away belongings.

The surprise of the suicide quickly turns to bewilderment.

Strengths for suicide prevention

There are other things the community, family, religious body, friends, and individuals can do to prevent suicide. Studies show that many people who don't act on suicidal thoughts, even though depressed, have developed protective mechanisms that often kick in during times of crisis.[1]

Some of these mechanisms include:

1. A responsibility to family.
2. Responsibility and love of children in the family.
3. Fear of social disapproval.
4. Moral objections to suicide.
5. Religiosity.
6. Social support.

One man in his late 40s, who has been treated for clinical depression for years and who has thoughts of suicide, would never do it because he says it would kill his 90-year-old mother. Fortunately, this man is receiving treatment and has help in dealing with his suicidal thoughts. Many others aren't reached in time, and despite families, religious affiliation, and moral turpitude, they still commit suicide. Still, those very systems and beliefs appear to prevent a certain number of other suicides.

Contacting the family physician can be a first step toward saving someone's life. If that option is not available, contact a suicide hotline in your area (see Resources).

Suicide warning signs

Signs of suicide may vary among different age groups. For instance, an older person may stop taking prescribed medications. A younger person may experience sudden changes in behavior.

The most common warning signs are:

1. Suicide threats.
2. Previous suicide attempts.
3. Statements revealing a desire to die.
4. Sudden changes in behavior such as withdrawal, apathy, moodiness, anger.
5. Depression, which may manifest itself in crying, sleeplessness, loss of appetite, and statements about hopelessness, helplessness, and worthlessness.
6. A preoccupation with and asking questions about death.
7. Trouble concentrating and making decisions.
8. Loss of interest in appearance.
9. Taking unnecessary risks.
10. Acquiring a weapon.
11. Failing to take prescribed medications or follow required diets.
12. Making final arrangements, such as giving away personal possessions.

13. Sudden appearance of happiness and calmness after a period of some of the characteristics listed above.

The role of guns in suicide

A very active sportswoman with a high-paying job told me recently that she would never keep a gun in the home for fear that she might use it on herself when she gets in one of her "blue moods."

"Have I ever had thoughts of suicide?" she said. "You bet. And I don't want something in easy reach that's going to make it easy when I'm in one of those moods."

"There is irrefutable evidence that the ready availability and accessibility of a firearm is a siren call to a quick and complete answer to the problems of someone who is suicidal. Suicides may occur on impulse when access to means is immediate and lethal. An increased use of firearms (available in the home) has been shown to be dramatically related to increased rates of youth suicide, to increased rates of young male African-American suicide, in particular. In contrast, where there are controls on the availability of firearms, there is strong evidence for decreased rates of suicide," says Berman, who is adamant about the relationship between guns in the home and suicide.

Berman's statements are validated by a majority of studies such as one by the Colorado Department of Public Health and Environment showing that of the 36 cases they studied, 67 percent of them used a gun obtained from their home; with adolescents, the figure was 72 percent.[2]

Each year, from 1991 to 1996, an average of 175 15-year-olds committed suicide with a firearm, and at least another 190 died from an accidental gunshot wound. In each of those same years, more than 1,000 15- to 19-year-olds killed themselves with guns.[3]

Further, recent evidence suggests that 75 percent of the firearms used in childhood and adolescent suicide attempts and accidental shootings are stored in the home of the victim or of a relative or friend. Even among adolescents with no apparent psychiatric disorder, loaded household firearms appear to be associated with a higher risk for suicide.

There has also been a concerted effort to encourage households with guns to provide locked and secure places of storage. Decreases in accidental firearm deaths have been attributed to the implementation of laws that hold gun owners responsible for how their guns are stored, in the event a child is injured with the gun. Experts from the National Rifle Association (NRA) to the American Academy of Pediatrics (AAP) agree that guns should be stored in a way that limits access by children.

However, the U.S. Surgeon General's report finds that even though it has been proposed that the rise in suicidal behavior among teen boys results from increased availability of firearms, and that the rate of suicide by firearms has increased more than by any other method, it notes that suicide rates also increased in Europe, Australia, and New Zealand, where suicide by firearms is rare.[4]

Another study shows how the Brady Handgun Violence Prevention Act has affected states that have implemented stricter gun controls (waiting periods and background checks). Suicides of persons aged 55 and older (an age group with one of the highest suicide rates) were reduced.[5]

The controversy over whether or not the availability of handguns contributes to suicide is certain to continue. In the meantime, it probably bodes well to follow the dictates from the NRA and the AAP, that guns should be stored away without access by children. Or to really play it safe, as Berman says, "Get the guns out of the home!"

Prevention targets all areas of society

Every aspect of the causes and prevention of suicide are being studied throughout the world, in towns, villages, and communities, in addition to government agencies and universities, in an effort to stem the tide of suicide and its tragic aftermath.

Many schools throughout the nation openly address suicide prevention in classrooms. It was once believed that discussing suicide encouraged suicide among the young, but that has been proven false.

Common thinking today is to teach young people that life is better than death, fostered in part after a federal court ruling in the 1980s when cluster suicides were making news. It was determined that school districts could be held liable if inadequate prevention measures contributed to a death.

Pilot suicide-prevention programs were established in school districts in two cities. When statistics were compiled in 1994, the teen suicide rates in those two cities had dropped from nearly triple the national average to 28 percent below the national average.[6]

Other studies have shown disparate results, some with improvements, and others with none. Some parental groups advocate for and some against the suicide prevention classes, so they are available in some districts and not in others.

When a teen suicide does occur

A variety of methods used in schools are available to educate students about suicide in the wake of a student suicide. The following is an example, based on methods developed at the Division of Child and Adolescent Psychiatry at the University of Minnesota Medical School, from the Substance Abuse and Mental Health Services Administration (SAMHSA), the Centers for Disease Control and Prevention, and from interviews with experts on suicide prevention.

1. Stress the idea that suicide is the result of dysfunctional behavior by a troubled personality.
2. Reduce identification with the actions of the deceased, and reaffirm that it was the fault of the person who committed suicide, not someone else's.
3. Emphasize what people can do to help each other rather than dwelling on the suicide.
4. Talk to the bereaved about what his or her concerns and stressors are about.
5. Don't glorify the death or prolong praises and tributes of the deceased.

6.   Get rid of available guns or drugs in the house, as depressed youths might use them in a careless moment.

It is clear from most studies that when people are suicidal it pays to confront the issue, offer to listen to the person, and seek additional help for him or her.

Children are particularly vulnerable to undiagnosed depression. "Kids don't articulate that they're depressed. A kid might not be conscious that he's moving toward suicide as would an adult. Their highs and lows are very different, and so they [parents] don't heed the signs," says Allen.

No category is exempt from suicide. Branches of the military have added suicide prevention programs. Psychologists have been placed on board naval vessels to deal with some of the unique shipboard issues. These issues can include loss of privacy, family problems created by long separations, and long work hours, all of which have manifested themselves in anger, depression, anxiety, and thoughts of suicide.[7] The United States Air Force trains officers and enlisted men that it's acceptable to seek psychological help with reducing suicide rates.[8]

Media guidelines

The media guidelines prepared by the CDC and AAS basically ask that the media and the parties affected by or involved in a suicide should "understand that a scientific basis exists for concern that news coverage of suicide may contribute to the causation of suicide."

The guidelines suggest that reporting a suicide should be concise and factual, and that the suicide contagion may be increased by presenting simplistic explanations for suicide. They state that in order to minimize the likelihood of suicide contagion:

1.   Reporting should be concise and factual.
2.   Excessive or sensational reporting of suicide in the news can lead to contagion.

3. Reporting technical aspects of the suicide isn't necessary
4. Suicide shouldn't be presented as an effective coping strategy
5. Suicide shouldn't be glorified
6. That expressions of grief, such as public eulogies and public memorials, should be minimized.[9]

The goals

The goals are many faceted when it comes to suicide. Prevention, of course, is the ideal. But all suicides can't be prevented. The goals also include working to make the community more healthful, and to rid itself of the stigma, taboos, and myths surrounding suicide. The clergy sometimes struggles with the concept of suicide, but in the meantime, gives comfort to its victims.

Once a suicide occurs, the deed is done and acceptance begins for the family and friends left behind. Whether we're the survivors, or the supports of the survivors, love and understanding must mingle with the debris of tragedy.

No one should have to hide grief with the thought in mind that society sets limits and bounds on it. Suicide will not disappear from the face of the earth, and neither will the attending grief. But we can lessen the ignorance surrounding it, and therefore become more sensitive to those who are struggling to continue their lives in the face of adversity.

Chapter Notes

Some of the chapter materials were first sent to me by universities and organizations in the form of press releases, but when possible, I have also supplied the source of published abstracts corresponding to the initial PR releases for those interested in reading the full report. The majority of material in the book, however, is from interviews, sometimes in tandem with research, and other mental health experts and survivors. Other materials are from public symposiums, briefings, addresses, and conventions.

Introduction:

1. Durkheim, E. *Suicide*. Glencoe, Illinois: Free Press, 1951.

Chapter 1:

1. Knieper, A.J. *The suicide survivor's grief and recovery.* Suicide and Life Threatening Behavior, 1999 Winter; 29(4): 353-64.

2. Bailley, S.E., et. al. *Survivors of suicide do grieve differently: empirical support for a common sense proposition.* Suicide and Life Threatening Behavior, 1999 Autumn; 29 (3): 256-71.

3. Pfeffer, C.R., et. al. *Child survivors of parental death from cancer or suicide: depressive and behavioral outcomes.* Psychooncology, 2000 Jan-Feb; 9 (1): 1-10.

4. Brent, D.A., et. al. *The impact of adolescent suicide on siblings and parents: a longitudinal follow-up.* Suicide and Life Threatening Behavior, 1996 Fall; 26 (3): 253-9.

5. van der Wal, J. Paper presented at the Second European Symposium on Suicidal Behavior, Edinburgh, May 29-June 1, 1988.

6. Wrobleski, A. *OMEGA: Journal of Death and Dying*, 15 (1984): 173-84. (interviewed Wrobleski).

7. Fawcett, J. M.D., et. al. *New Hope for People with Bipolar Disorder.* Roseville, California: Prima Publishing, 2000. Pgs. 55-62.

8. Simpson, E. *Orphans Real and Imaginary.* New York; Weidenfield & Nicholson, 1987.

9. Sekaer, C. *American Journal of Psychotherapy,* 41 (1987): 201-19. (interviewed Sekaer).

10. Cutcliffe, J.R. *Hope, counselling and complicated bereavement reactions.* Journal of Advanced Nursing 1998 Oct; 28 (4): 754-61.

11. Range, L.M., et. al. *Does writing about the bereavement lessen grief following sudden, unintentional death?* Death Studies 2000 Mar; 24 (2): 115-34.

12. Szanto, K., et.al. *Suicidal ideation in elderly bereaved: the role of complicated grief.* Suicide and Life Threatening Behavior, 1997 Summer; 27 (2): 194-207.

13. Romanoff, B.D. and M. Terenzio. *Rituals and the grieving process.* Death Studies, 1998 Dec; 22 (8): 697-711.

14. Brave Heart, M.Y. and L.M. DeBruyn. *The American Indian Holocaust: healing historical unresolved grief.* American Indian and Alaskan Native Mental Health Resource, 1998; 8 (2): 56-78.

15. Shneidman, E. *Suicide and Life Threatening Behavior,* 15 (1985): 51-55.

Chapter 2:

All interviews with survivors.

Chapter 3:

1. Farmer, R.D.T., *British Journal of Psychiatry,* 153 (1988); 16-20.

2. Peruzzi, N. Ph.D., of MyPsych.com, a division of Hemisphere Healthcare and B. Bongar, Ph.D., of the Pacific Graduate School of Psychology and Stanford University School of Medicine, surveyed 500 psychologists nationwide. Participants were presented with 48 risk factors for suicide and were asked to rate the factors from low importance to critical or high importance. Press release. Reported in the December, 1999 issue of *Professional Psychology: Research and Practice,* published by the American Psychological Association.

3. Fourth International Obsessive Compulsive Disorder Conference, Feb. 10-12 2000.

4. Johns Hopkins Medical Institutions. Press release, 1 Sep. 98. *First Significant Genetic Evidence for Schizophrenia Susceptibility.* Also reported in the August, 1998 issue of *Nature Genetics.*

5. Rush-Presbyterian Medical Center. *Suicide an Inherited Trait?* Press release. April, 1996.

6. Shneidman, E. *Voice of Death.* New York: Harper & Row, 1980.

7. Lester, D. *Differences in content of suicide notes by age and method.* Perceptual Motor Skills, 1998 Oct; 87 (2): 530.

8. Ho, T.P., et. al. *Suicide notes: what do they tell us?* Acta Psychiatry Scandenavia, 1998 Dec; 98 (6): 467-73.

9. *British Medical Journal* 2000; 321: 528 (2 September). Suicides in Japan reach a record high.

10. O'Connor, R.C., et. al. *A thematic analysis of suicide notes.* Crisis, 1999; 20 (3): 106-14.

11. New England Journal of Medicine, 1986 Vol., 315 No.11: 685-9.

12. Gould, M.S. professor of psychiatry and public health, Columbia University, and scientific researcher at the New York Psychiatric Institute. *Psychological Autopsy of Cluster Suicides in Adolescents.* Early evaluation of project funded by the National Institute of Mental Health from research covering 53 suicide clusters involving 208 school-age children. Material from study was being evaluated in 2000. (Interviewed Gould)

13. Jessen, G. and B.F. Jessen. *Postponed suicide death? Suicides around birthdays and major public holiday.* Suicide and Life Threatening Behavior, 1999 Autumn; 29 (3): 272-83.

14. Nishi, M., et. al. *Relationship between suicide and holidays.* Journal of Epidemiology, 2000 Sep; 10 (5): 317-20.

15. Morken, G. and O.M. Linaker. *Seasonal variation of violence in Norway.* American Journal of Psychiatry, 2000 Oct; 157 (10): 1674-8.

16. Gaugelin, M. *How Atmospheric Conditions Affect Your Health.* New York: Stein and Day, 1971.

17. Russell, D. and F. Judd. *Why are men killing themselves? A look at the evidence.* Australian Family Physician, 1999 Aug; 28 (8): 791-5.

18. Rabinowitz, F. and S. Cochran. *Men and Depression: Clinical and Empirical Perspectives.* San Diego: Academic Press, 2000.

(Also interviewed Rabinowitz). University of Redlands, press release, 20-Sep-00 (Interviewed Rabinowitz)

19. Thomas, C.B. *What becomes of medical students: the dark side.* Johns Hopkins Medical Journal, 1976 May; 138 (5): 185-95.

20. Alexander, B.H., et.al. *The health-related effects of the operating room environment are unclear. The authors compared mortality risks of anesthesiologists to those of internal medicine physicians between 1979 and 1995.* Anesthesiology, 2000 Oct; 93 (4): 922-30.

21. Hem, E., et al. *The prevalence of suicidal ideation and suicidal attempts among Norwegian physicians. Results from a cross-sectional survey of a nationwide sample.* European Psychiatry, 2000 May; 15 (3): 183-9.

22. Kashani, J.H. and M. Priesmeyer. *Differences in depressive symptoms and depression among college students.* American Journal of Psychiatry, 1983 Aug; 140 (8): 108 1-2.

Chapter 4:

1. Chamberlin, J. Monitor on Psychology (tabloid). Volume 31, No. 1, January 2000.

2. Breitbart, M.D. and S. William. *Untreated Depression and Hopelessness and Death Wish.* Memorial Sloan-Kettering Cancer Center. Press release. December 9, 2000.

3. Stark, E. and A. H. Flitcraft. Spouse Abuse. Working paper solicited and edited by the Violence Epidemiology Branch, Center for Health Promotion and Education, Centers for Disease Control, Atlanta, Georgia, as a background document for the Surgeon General's Workshop on Violence and Public Health, Leesburg, Virginia, October 1985.

4. Counts, D.A. *Female suicide and wife abuse in cross cultural perspective.* Suicide and Life Threatening Behavior, 1987; 17 (3): 194-204.

5. Harwood, D.M., et. al. *Suicide in older people: mode of death, demographic factors, and medical contact before death.* International Journal of Geriatric Psychiatry, 2000 Aug; 15 (8): 736-43.

6. Uncapher, H. and P.A. Arean. *Physicians are less willing to treat suicidal ideation in older patients.* Journal of the American Geriatric Society, 2000 Feb; 48 (2): 188-92.

7. Rihmer, Z., et. al. *Depression and suicide on Gotland. An intensive study of all suicides before and after a depression-training programme for general practitioners.* Journal of Affective Disorders, 1995 Dec 18; 35 (4): 147-52.

8. American Heart Association. *Feeling Down Could Raise the Risk for Heart Disease.* Press release, October 2000. Also reported in the Oct. 2000 issue of *Circulation: Journal of the American Heart Association* 10-Oct-00.

9. 1999: Mental Health: A Report from the Surgeon General.

10. Bagley, C. and A.R. D'Augelli. *Suicidal behaviour in gay, lesbian, and bisexual youth.* BMJ 2000; 320:1 617-1618 (17 June), Editorials.

11. Bagley, C. and P. Tremblay. *Suicidal behaviors in homosexual and bisexual males.* Crisis 1997; 18 (1): 24-34.

12. American Psychiatric Association. Press release No. 00-32 June 19, 2000.

13. Green, L., et. al. *HIV, childbirth and suicidal behaviour: a review.* Journal of Hospital Medicine, 2000 May; 61 (5): 311-4.

14. Beautrais, A.L. *Methods of youth suicide in New Zealand: trends and implications for prevention.* Australian-New Zealand Journal of Psychiatry, 2000 Jun; 34 (3): 413-9.

15. Birmaher, B., et al. *Childhood and adolescent depression: a review of the past 10 years. Part I.* American Academy of Child and Adolescent Psychiatry, 1996, Nov; 35 (11): 1427-39

16. American Psychiatric Association, Release No. 00-42 26-Sep-2000. *Most Depressed Teens Do Not Get Treatment.* Also, October 2000, American Journal of Psychiatry. (Interviewed Paul Rohde, PhD, one of researchers)

17. McGarvey, E.L., et. al. *Incarcerated adolescents' distress and suicidality in relation to parental bonding styles.* Crisis, 1999; 20 (4): 164-70.

18. American Psychiatric Association. *Traumatic Grief Makes Young Adults Five Times More Vulnerable to Thoughts of Suicide.* Nov. 22, 1999 Release No. 99-36. Also in the December, 1999 issue of the American Journal of Psychiatry.

19. Salk, L., et. al. *Relationship of maternal and perinatal conditions to eventual adolescent suicide.* Lancet, 1985 Mar 16; 1 (8429): 624-7.

20. Workman, C.G. and M. Prior. *Depression and suicide in young children.* Issues in Comprehensive Pediatric Nursing, 1997 Apr-Jun; 20 (2): 125-32.

21. Workman, C.G. and M. Prior. *Depression and suicide in young children.* Issues in Comprehensive Pediatric Nursing, 1997 Apr-Jun; 20 (2): 125-32.

22. Svetaz, M.V., et. al. *Adolescents with learning disabilities: risk and protective factors associated with emotional well-being: findings from the national longitudinal study of adolescent health.* Adolescent Health, 2000 Nov; 27 (5): 340-8.

23. Holmes, M.D. and William C. University of Pennsylvania Medical Center. Press release, 1-Dec-98 *Sexual Abuse of Boys Is More Common Than Believed.*

24. National Center for Injury Prevention & Control. *Homicide and Suicide Among Native Americans, 1979-1992.* Violence Surveillance Summary Series, No. 2.

25. Remarks by Donna E. Shalala, Secretary of Health and Human Services. Native American Health and Welfare Conference, Tucson, Arizona, October 23, 1998. Challenges of Native American Health and Welfare for the next Millennium.

26. *Australasian Psychiatry*, v.5 no.5 Oct 1997: 231-232.

27. Brave Heart, M.Y. and L.M. DeBruyn. *The American Indian Holocaust: healing historical unresolved grief.* American Indian and Alaskan Native Mental Health Resource 1998; 8 (2): 56-78.

28. Peters, K.D., et.al. (1998). Deaths: Final data for 1996. National Vital Statistics Report, 47(9) Hyattsville, MD: National Center for Health Statistics. DHHS Publication No. (PHS) 99-1120 (p. 79, Table 24).

29. The briefing was sponsored by the Suicide Prevention Advocacy Network (SPAN), a group started by people who had lost family members to suicide. SPAN has received a research grant from the Center for Mental Health Services (CMHS) to identify the best suicide-prevention practices. The new center is affiliated with the Trauma Institute of the University of Nevada School of Medicine, the Critical Illness and Trauma Foundation, Inter-mountain Regional Emergency Medical Services, and the Coordinating Council and American Association of Suicidology.

30. Zubieta, J. M.D., Ph.D. assistant professor of psychiatry and radiology, University of Michigan. *Evidence of Brain Chemistry Abnormalities in Bipolar Disorder.* Press release, 28-Sep-00.

   Zubieta, J.K., et. al. *High vesicular monoamine transporter binding in asymptomatic bipolar I disorder: sex differences and cognitive correlates*. American Journal of Psychiatry, 2000 Oct; 157 (10): 1619-28.

31. Fawcett, J., M.D., et. al. *New Hope for People with Bipolar Disorder.* Roseville, California: Prima Publishing, 2000. Pg. 155.

Chapter 5:

1. Burzun, J. *From Dawn to Decadence*. New York: Harper Collins Publishers, 2000. Pgs. 222-223.

2. Cass, A.M., et. al. of the Center for Psychological Studies at Nova Southeastern University in Fort Lauderdale, FL., presenters. American Psychological Association. *High Pay, Depression Linked in Study of Stockbrokers*. Press release Aug. 2000. American Psychological Association Convention, Aug. 2000.

3. *Menninger Perspective*, 4 (1988):5.

4. Press release from the World Health Organization (WHO). Also available at *http://www.who.ch/*

Beijing, 12 November 1999. To ease the "burden" of mental disorders and neurological illnesses, currently affecting some 400 million people worldwide, the Director-General of the World Health Organization (WHO), Dr Gro Harlem Brundtland, launched here today WHO's new Global Strategies for Mental Health. The strategies are aimed at improving the population coverage and quality of psychiatric and neurological care throughout the world, particularly in developing countries. Based on the DALY, "Disability-Adjusted Life Years"—jointly developed by WHO, the World Bank, and Harvard University. The DALY measures the overall burden of a disease by combining, on the one hand, the years of potential life lost due to premature death from the disease and, on the other, the years of productive life lost due to the disability produced by the condition.

5. Washington, D.C.—One hundred and three medicines are in the pipeline to help the more than 50 million Americans who suffer from some form of mental illness, according to a newly released survey by the Pharmaceutical Research and Manufacturers of America (PhRMA).

6. Williams, R.A. and P. Strasser. University of Michigan. Press release. *Disabled by Depression, Costs, Causes*. Nov. 3, 1999. Also in the November, 1999 issue of *American Association of Occupational Health Nurses Journal*.

7. Pharmaceutical Research and Manufacturers of America (PhRMA). Press release, 21-Jun-00. 103 *Medicines in Development for Mental Illnesses.*

8. University of Miami School of Medicine. *Students' Reaction to Posttraumatic Stress, Depression, and Social Support after Hurricane Andrew.* Press release, May 1997.

9. Furberg, C., M.D., Ph.D., a professor of public health science at Wake Forest University. American Heart Association. *Feeling Down Could Raise the Risk for Heart Disease.* Press release, Oct. 2000. Also reported in the Oct. 2000 issue of Circulation: American Heart Association journal, 10-Oct-00.

10. Sarrel, P.M. *Psychosexual effects of menopause: role of androgens.* American Journal of Obstetrics and Gynecology, 1999 Mar;180(3 Pt 2):S319-24. Dell, D.L., and D.E. Stewart. *Menopause and mood. Is depression linked with hormone changes?* Postgraduate Medicine, 2000 Sep 1; 108 (3): 34-6, 39-43

11. Burt, V.K., et. al. Depressive symptoms in the perimenopause: prevalence, assessment, and guidelines for treatment. *Harvard Revue of Psychiatry*, 1998 Sep-Oct; 6 (3): 121-32

12. Dell, D.L. and D.E. Stewart. *Menopause and mood. Is depression linked with hormone changes?* Postgraduate Medicine, 2000 Sep 1; 108 (3): 34-6, 39-43

13. American Psychological Association. *Researchers Offer Reasons Why Women Experience Depression More than Men Do.* Press release, Oct. 31, 1999. Also, Journal of Personality and Social Psychology, November, 1999.

14. Zubieta, J., M.D., Ph.D. *Evidence of Brain Chemistry Abnormalities in Bipolar Disorder.* Press release, University of Michigan 28-Sep-00.

15. Mayberg, H., M.D. Rotman Research Institute, Baycrest Centre for Geriatric Care, University of Toronto. Press release, April 1999. (Interviewed Mayberg)

16. Grazyna, R. *Brain Changes in Depression.* Press release, May 4, 1999. University of Mississippi Medical Center. Also in the May, 1999 issue of the journal, *Biological Psychiatry.*

17. Washington University School of Medicine in St. Louis. *Brain Atrophy Found in Patients With Recurrent Depression.* Press release, Aug. 1996. Also reported in Proceedings of the National Academy of Sciences, Vol. 93 (9): 3908-3913, April 30, 1996.

18. American Heart Association. *Being chronically "blue" raises risk of heart attack, all-cause mortality.* Press release, May 31, 1996. Also reported in the June, 1996 issue of *Circulation*.

19. Carney, R.M., et. al. *Change in heart rate and heart rate variability during treatment for depression in patients with coronary heart disease.* Psychosomatic Medicine 2000 Sep-Oct; 62 (5): 639-47. (Interviewed Carney)

20. Lustman, P.J., et. al. *Depression and poor glycemic control: a meta-analytic review of the literature.* Diabetes Care 2000 Jul; 23 (7): 934-42. (Interviewed Carney)

21. Juel, K., et. al. *Mortality and causes of death among Danish medical doctors 1973-1992.* International Journal of Epidemiology, International Journal of Epidemiology, 1999 Jun; 28 (3): 456-60.

22. Lindeman, S., et. al. *Treatment of mental disorders in seven physicians committing suicide.* Crisis, 1999; 20 (2): 86-9.

23. Isacsson, G. Acta Psychiatrica Scandinavica, 2000 Aug; 102 (2): 113-7.

Chapter 6:

1. Dublin, L. *Suicide: A Sociological and Statistical Study.* New York: Ronald Press Co., 1963.

2. Sumner, W.G. *Folkways.* Boston: Ginn & Co, 1906.

3. National Vital Statistics Report, Vol. 47, No. 19, June 30, 1999: Center for Disease Control.

4. World Health Organization Report, 1999. Brundtland Unveils New WHO Global Strategies for Mental Health, Sees Poverty as a Major Obstacle to Mental Well Being. Beijing, 12 November 1999. To ease the "burden" of mental disor-

ders and neurological illnesses, currently affecting some 400 million people worldwide, the Director-General of the World Health Organization (WHO), Dr. Gro Harlem Brundtland, launched here today WHO's new Global Strategies for Mental Health.

5. Nisbet, P.A., et. al. *The effect of participation in religious activities on suicide versus natural death in adults 50 and older.* Journal of Nervous and Mental Disorders, 2000 Aug; 188 (8): 543-6.

6. Sullivan, A.D., et. al., *Legalized physician-assisted suicide in Oregon—the second year.* New England Journal of Medicine, 2000 Feb 24; 342 (8): 598-604.

7. Editorial in the December 4, 2000 edition of *American Medical News.*

Chapter 7:

1. Brodie, G. *Death Studies.* 12 (1988): 147-71.

2. Ryn, Z., M.D. *Suicide and Life Threatening Behavior.* 16 (1986): 419-433.

3. Hewett, J.H. *After Suicide.* Philadelphia: Westminster Press, 1980.

4. Encyclopedia of Religion. Editor in chief Mircea Eliade. "Suicide (Buddhism and Confucianism)." New York: Macmillan, vol. 14 p.129.

5. Khan, M.M. and H. Reza. *The pattern of suicide in Pakistan.* Crisis, 2000; 21 (1): 31-5.

Chapter 8:

1. Malone, K.M., M.D. *Reasons for Living Can Prevent Suicide During Depression.* Press release, No. 00-31, June 16, 2000, American Psychiatric Association. Also *American Journal of*

Psychiatry. June 19, 2000. [Protective Factors Against Suicidal Acts in Major Depression: Reason For Living," by., et. al., p1084].

2. Shah, S, et. al. *Adolescent suicide and household access to firearms in Colorado: results of a case-control study*. Adolescent Health, 2000 Mar; 26 (3): 157-63.

3. Azrael, D., et.al. *Are household firearms stored safely? It depends on whom you ask.* Pediatrics, Vol. 106 No. 3 September 2000, p. e31.

4. 1999: Mental Health: A Report From the Surgeon General.

5. Ludwig, J. Ph.D. and P.J. Cook, Ph.D. *Homicide and Suicide Rates Associated With Implementation of the Brady Handgun Violence Prevention Act.* JAMA. 2000; 284: 585-591.

6. Nazario, S. *Los Angeles Times*. 3-10-1997.

7. Monitor On-line (American Psychological Association). *Navy to put more psychologists on board.* Volume 30, Number 7 July/August 1999.

8. Monitor On-line (American Psychological Association). *Military suicide-prevention program reduces the stigma of seeking help*. Volume 30, Number 10 November 1999.

9. Centers for Disease Control. Programs for the prevention of suicide among adolescents and young adults; and suicide contagion and the reporting of suicide: Recommendations from a national workshop. MMWR 1994; 43 (No. RR-6).

Bibliography

Barzun, J. *From Dawn to Decadence*. New York: Harper Collins, 2000. Pgs. 222-223.

Dublin, L. *Suicide: A Sociological and Statistical Study*. New York: Ronald Press Co., 1963.

Fawcett, M.D., J., et al. *New Hope for People with Bipolar Disorder*. Roseville, Calif.: Prima Publishing, 2000.

Kastenbaum, R.& B. *Encyclopedia of Death*. Phoenix, Arizona: Oryz Press, 1989.

Rabinowitz, F. and S. Cochran. *Men and Depression: Clinical and Empirical Perspectives*. San Diego: Academic Press, 2000.

Shneidman, E. *Voices of Death*. New York: Harper & Row, 1980.

Simpson, E. *Orphans Real and Imaginary*. New York: Weidenfield & Nicholson, 1987.

Stone, G. *Suicide and Attempted Suicide*. New York: Carroll & Graf Publishers Inc., 1999.

Sumner, W.G. *Folkways*. Boston: Ginn & Co., 1906.

Resources

American Association for Geriatric Psychiatry
7910 Woodmont Ave., Suite 11050
Bethesda, MD 20815
301/654-7850
www.aagpgpa.org

American Association for Marriage and Family Therapy
1133 15th St. NW
Washington, DC 20005
202/452-0109
www.aamft.org

American Association of Suicidology
4201 Connecticut Ave., NW, Suite 408
Washington, DC 20008
202/237-2280
Fax: 202/237-2282
www.suicidology.org

American Foundation for Suicide Prevention
120 Wall St., 22nd Fl.
New York, NY 10005
888/357-2377
Fax: 212/363-6237
www.afsp.org

American Psychiatric Association
1400 K St., NW
Washington, DC 20005
888/357-7924
www.psych.org

American Psychological Association
750 First St., NE
Washington, DC 20002
202/336-5700
800/374-3120
www.apa.org

Centers for Disease Control and Prevention

Programs for the prevention of suicide among adolescents and young adults; and suicide contagion and the reporting of suicide: Recommendations from a national workshop. MMWR 1994; 43 (No. RR-6). Copies of the MMWR are available at $3.00 each from:

Massachusetts Medical Society
C.S.P.O. Box 9120
Waltham, MA 02254-9120

National Center for Injury Prevention and Control
www.cdc.gov/ncipc

Constructive Living/Morita/Naikon
David K. Reynolds
dkreynolds@juno.com
www.click.or.jp/ ~ dkr

ToDo Institute
P.O. Box 874
Middlebury, VT 05753
802/453-4440
Fax: 802/352-1050
73002.2511@compuserve.com
www.anamorph.com/todo/institute.html

Cognitive therapy

www.Rapidcognitivetherapy.com
www.metathoughts.com

Depression and Related Affective Disorders, Association
The John Hopkins Hospital, Meyer 3-181
600 North Wolfe St.
Baltimore, MD 21287
410/955-4647
Fax: 410/614-3241
www.med.jhu.edu/drada

International Association for Suicide Prevention (IASP)
International Association Suicide Prevention,
Central Administrative Office, Rush Presbyterian, St. Luke's
Medical Center
Rush University
1725 West Harrison St., Suite 955
Chicago, IL 60612-3824
IASP@aol.com

Mental Health: A Report of the Surgeon General. 1999
www.surgeongeneral.gov/library/mentalhealth/home.html

National Alliance for the Mentally Ill
2107 Wilson Blvd., Suite 300
Arlington, VA 22201
703/524-7600
800/950-6264
Fax: 703/524-9094
www.nami.org

National Depressive and Manic-Depressive Association
(National DMDA)
730 N. Franklin St., Suite 501
Chicago, IL 60610
800/826-3632
Fax: 312/642-7243
www.ndmda.org

National Foundation for Depressive Illness
P.O. Box 2257
New York, NY 10116
800/239-1265
www.depression.org

National Institute of Mental Health
6001 Executive Blvd.
Bethesda, MD 20892
800/421-4211
www.nimh.nih.gov

National Institute of Mental Health
 Suicide ResearchConsortium
www.nimh.nih.gov/research/suicide.htm

National Mental Health Association
1201 Prince St.
Alexandria, VA 22314
800/969-6642
800-228-1114 to obtain information on clinical depression or to locate a local site that offers free, confidential, one-on-one depression screenings year-round.
Fax: 703/684-5968
www.nmha.org

Suicide Information and Education Center
siec@siec.ca
#201, 1615 - 10th Ave. SW
Calgary, Alberta   Canada   T3C 0J7
403/245-3900
Fax: 403/245-0299
www.suicideinfo.ca/siec.htm

World Health Organization
http://www.who.int/mental_health/Suicide/

For help locating a local hotline, or for bereavement groups

The National "YOUTH" Crisis Helpline:
800/999-9999

National Resource Center for Suicide Prevention and Aftercare:
404/256-9797

Youth Crisis Hotline. Counseling and referrals for teens in crisis
800/448-4663

National Directory of Support Groups for Survivors of Suicide
www.suicidology.org/survivorssupport.htm

Or for more information, contact:
American Association of Suicidology
4201 Connecticut Ave., NW Suite 408
Washington, DC 20008
202/237-2280

Index

A

Addiction,
  alcohol, 86, 165
  drug, 86, 165
American Association of
Suicidology, 70, 90, 174
American Foundation for
Suicide Prevention, 142
Anger, survivors', 49, 50, 62
Autism, 17

B

Bereavement,
  emotions of, 24, 32
  rituals of, 44-45

Bipolar disorder, 33, 63, 75, 77,
  103, 112, 116
Blame, 39, 79, 129
Buddhism, 135, 137, 138,
  155-157

C

Celebrities, suicide by, 76,
  95-96, 103
Centers for Disease Control
  (CDC), 90, 102, 174
Christianity, 136-138, 150-155
Clusters, suicide, 91-92
Condolences, offering of, 25

D

Depression,
  among the elderly, 104-106,
    122
  as cause of suicide, 16, 27,
    51, 53, 77, 83, 86, 101, 103,
    115-118
  associated with the grieving
    process, 37
  definition of, 118-119
  factors contributing to, 116,
    124-125
  physiological aspects,
    122-124
  symptoms of, 119-122
  treatments of, 37, 120, 126-134
Durkheim, Emile, 16, 138

E

Egyptians, ancient, 135
Euthanasia, 143-146
Exercise, 37, 133-134

G

Greece, ancient, 135-136
Grief, survivors', 19, 23, 27,
    28-31
  characteristics of, 33, 37
  children's experience of,
    36-37
  need for, 34
  working through, 41-46, 73
Guilt, survivors', 27, 38-41, 50,
    60, 147
Guns, suicide and, 171-172

H

Hinduism, 137, 138, 159-160
Holidays, suicide and, 93
Homosexuality, suicide and,
    106-107
Hypocrites, 115

I

Imaging, 45-46
Insanity, 84
International Association for
Prevention of Suicide (IAPS),
    142
Islam, 157-159

J

Judaism,148-150

M

Media, coverage of suicide in,
    174-175
Men, suicide by, 94-95
Monoamines, 123
Myths, suicide, 75-99

N

National Alliance for the
Mentally Ill, 90
National Institute of Mental
Health (NIMH), 87, 104, 116,
    128, 140
Notes, suicide, 89-90

O

Obsessive compulsive disorder (OCD), 86, 116

R

Rates, suicide
among age groups
adolescents, 87, 90, 91-92, 101, 107-108
children 87, 108-110
elderly, 87, 101, 104-106
middle-aged, 87
young adults, 87, 91-92, 101
among races, 96-98, 110-111
among religions, 99
among socioeconomic classes, 98-99
by country, 102, 142
by U.S. geographic areas, 111
during holiday seasons, 93
in the 20th century, 141
related to gender, 94-95
related to time of day, 93-94
Rome, ancient, 135-136

S

Schizophrenia, 17, 77, 86, 103, 112, 116
Shneidman, Edwin, 46, 89
Suicide
attempts at, 88
criminal act of, 138
definition of, 16
family member's
child's, 51-52, 69-74
parent's, 48-50, 58-63
sibling's, 63-68
spouse's, 53-58
fears associated with, 33
genetic predisposition for, 27, 86
people affected by, 76-78
prevention of, 169-170, 172-173
reasons for, 26, 77, 85, 101
risk factors for, 82, 103-104
societal attitudes and 139-142
stages of, 169
threats of, 80, 83
warning signs of, 82, 164, 170
Support groups, 23, 52, 56, 69, 139, 140

T

Taboos, 143
Television, suicide and, 90
Therapy,
behavioral, 128-130
cognitive, 129-130
drug, 131-133
grief, 19
interpersonal, 128-129
Morita, 130-131
Thoughts, suicidal, 38, 87

W

Women, suicide by, 94-95
World Health Organization (WHO), 101, 116, 141-142

About the
Author

Rita Robinson is an award-winning journalist specializing in health and psychology. Author of 10 books, she has also been published in more than 1,000 magazines on three continents. She conducts writers' workshops for colleges, writers' organizations, and other professional groups. She lives in Southern California.